I0731760

Saying I Love You Forever

New Adult Sweet Romance Series, Volume 3

Ellie J. Adams

Published by Wheelhouse Publishers LLC, 2020.

Copyright

Wheelhouse Publishers, LLC
    c/o Registered Agents, Inc.
    82 Wendell Avenue, Suite 100
    Pittsfield, MA 01201
    To learn more about Wheelhouse Publishers, visit:
    wheelhousepublishers.com

Prologue

I gasped for breath and fought back tears. I felt like I had been punched in the gut by the shocking news that we had just received. If it were true, it would shake the very foundation of the life Brandon and I were building together. In fact, it could quite possibly destroy any hopes we had of spending the rest of our lives together.

Gina Arlotti wanted more than to disrupt a wedding; she wanted to destroy Brandon's life. She wanted to deny me a life with him. Gina wanted to take everything we had for herself.

A week before, I had no idea who Gina Arlotti was. A week before, my life looked a lot different than it did in that moment. A week before, Brandon and I were celebrating the fourth anniversary of our first date and making plans for the future. A future threatened by Gina Arlotti's shocking news.

Chapter 1

Brandon Mitchell was a CEO with an almost rock star status. He held the title of most eligible bachelor and was considered one of the most handsome men in the world. Such a station in life allowed Brandon to date many beautiful women. Actresses, supermodels, even royalty. Ten years ago, one of those women had been Italian supermodel Gina Arlotti. It was a brief relationship Brandon had long forgotten.

There had been many women before and since Gina Arlotti. Four years ago, one of those women had been Ashley Sullivan. But Ashley was different from Gina and all the others. Brandon fell in love with her and their romance had blossomed. He was even planning on asking Ashley to marry him.

Brandon thought about his proposal as he drove his Aston Martin DB8 along the Pacific coast toward the Lusso Resort and Spa in Santa Barbara, California. The Lusso Resort was a special place for Brandon and Ashley. They had their first date at Francesca's restaurant located at Lusso's, followed by a long and romantic walk along the beach.

Brandon's daydreaming of their first date nearly caused him to clip the curb as he pulled up to Lusso's main entrance. Brandon removed his New York Yankees baseball cap and placed it on the passenger seat. He ran his fingers through his short, jet black hair. He left the Aston Martin with the valet and entered the hotel lobby.

Even dressed in faded jeans, a navy blue T-shirt, and an old pair of tennis sneakers, Brandon caught the attention of most of the women in the lobby. His six foot two inch athletic frame was pure muscle. His face was tanned and classically handsome. Brandon's lips were soft and full. The start of a five o shadow only added to his appeal.

Brandon crossed the lobby to Francesca's restaurant.

"Good afternoon, Mr. Mitchell," greeted the host.

"Good afternoon. I wanted to check on my reservation for this evening," said Brandon.

The host checked the reservation system. He gave a smile as he pulled up Brandon's reservation.

"Yes, everything looks to be in order." The host swiveled the computer screen him. Brandon looked over the reservation notes.

"Do you wish to make any changes?" asked Francesca's host.

"No. Everything looks good," replied Brandon.

"Excellent. We will make sure it is a perfect evening for you and Miss Sullivan."

"Thank you," said Brandon.

"Thank you, sir," said the host.

Brandon left Francesca's and headed to his suite in the resort. Ashley knew about dinner, but she had no idea what Brandon had planned. It was the fourth anniversary of their first date and Brandon wanted it to be a special evening.

As he opened the door to the suite, Brandon saw Ashley stretched out on a patio chair in shorts and a casual blouse. He never got over how great she looked without even trying. Brandon loved Ashley more than words could express. He never thought he would fall in love and want to spend a month with someone, let alone the rest of his life.

Ashley looked over at Brandon and smiled as he crossed the living room toward the open French doors. A warm breeze with a hint of the Pacific Ocean greeted Brandon as he moved toward the outside. Beyond the patio was the beach where they took their romantic stroll four years before and where they would share their special evening in just a few hours.

Chapter 2

I was already enjoying the fourth anniversary of our first date and it promised to get even better. The evening air was warm as Brandon led me along one of Lusso's oceanfront paths. It was in the general direction of Francesca's but not toward the restaurant entrance.

"I thought we were having dinner at Francesca's?" I asked.

"We are," replied Brandon. "With a little bit of a twist."

"A twist?"

"Yes. Be patient."

As we rounded the bend, I could see an elegantly set table for two on a private patio overlooking the Pacific Ocean. A waiter was standing next to the table.

"Good evening, Mr. Mitchell, Ms. Sullivan," greeted the waiter as we approached.

Brandon held out my chair for me and I sat. He then sat opposite me. The waiter poured us each a glass of our favorite red wine and left us with menus.

"This is absolutely lovely," I said.

The table had beautiful white linens and Francesca's fine place settings. The table and patio area was lit completely by candlelight. A string quartet appeared and sat off in the corner of the patio. They played softly in the background.

I glanced over at the quartet. I then took it all in. The ocean, the candlelight, the linens, the fine dinnerware, and, of course, Brandon. The love of my life. He was still my "Mr. Handsome CEO." That is how my best friend Chelsea had often referred to Brandon when he was my celebrity crush.

Brandon's dark hair was neatly trimmed and perfectly combed in place. His tanned skin glowed in the candlelight. His gorgeous blue eyes twinkled with wonder and excitement. Brandon's smile was warm and every bit as captivating as I remembered it being when we first met.

Brandon was wearing one of his favorite double-breasted navy blue suits. He had a crisp white dress shirt and a blue tie to match the suit. I was wearing a black sleeveless evening gown with a deep neckline. Underneath, I wore a strapless black lace bra and matching panties.

"Brandon, sweetie, this all so wonderful."

"It is the fourth anniversary of our first date."

Brandon smiled broadly. I loved the way his mouth curled upward and formed two wonderful dimples. I also thought that he had the most perfect lips. Perfect for kissing.

"I'm just so glad to be here tonight. Of course, being anywhere with you is wonderful. We didn't have to fly cross country for our anniversary dinner," I said.

"We don't get here as much as I would like, so I figured this gave us a good excuse to take a little detour from our business trip to Los Angeles. Ashley, this is such a special place for us. That first evening together changed my life. It merits a grand celebration."

"Well, you have outdone yourself. I hope the after dinner celebration can live up to the dinner hype," I said with a seductive look as I took a sip of my wine.

"Oh, I can promise you that it will," replied Brandon.

"Very sure of yourself," I said.

"According to my girlfriend, I have a stellar track record."

"Yes. You do."

The waiter returned and took our order. We hadn't even bothered looking at our menus. We both ordered the Chicken Parmesan. It was what we always ordered when we came to Francesca's.

The string quartet played. The waiter refilled our wine glasses. A gentle breeze swept across the patio. Brandon and I were lost in each other's eyes. It was a wonderfully romantic evening.

"How do you think the Adele acquisition will go tomorrow?" I asked.

"I thought we agreed that we wouldn't talk business tonight," Brandon responded.

"I know. But I don't plan on doing much talking later. And the meeting is early in the morning."

"Ashley, look around you. Who cares about the acquisition of Adele?"

"Who cares? Well, you certainly are not sounding at all like the CEO that I know."

"I have far more important things on my mind tonight," said Brandon.

"Like what?" I asked.

"Like this Chicken Parm," said Brandon as the waiter arrived with our dinner.

"Very funny," I said.

"Anything else?" asked the waiter.

"No, thank you. Everything looks wonderful," replied Brandon to the waiter.

The waiter nodded and then retreated from the patio. Brandon cut into his chicken and took a bite. He had a satisfied look that he only truly got from great food, great wine, and spending time with me, and not necessarily in that order.

"Okay, now that you have experienced the rapture of delight from your first bite, let's chat a little about tomorrow," I pressed.

Jacqueline acquiring *Adele* was the biggest decision that Davenport Media had made in years. The news was all the buzz in the fashion industry. How could Brandon not want to discuss it?

"Okay. But just until we finish dinner. By the time we get to dessert, we are done with any talk of business until tomorrow morning. Agreed?"

"Agreed," I said.

"I think everything should go smoothly. Adele has a great staff. They will complement our Jacqueline staff very well. Having an office here will help us more effectively cover the west coast fashion world and related entertainment industry," said Brandon.

"I certainly hope that we will be keeping Lauren Caldwell, Ronald Vargas, and the social media staff," I said.

"Even though they tried to steal you away?"

Lauren Caldwell was the Vice President of Human Resources at *Adele* and Ronald Vargas was their Vice President of Business Development. A few years ago they had offered me a job at *Adele* to run their Digital and Social Media department. It was during a time when my future with Brandon was very much in doubt. The offer was extremely attractive. But Brandon followed me to California to win me back.

"Brandon, that was business. I stayed at *Jacqueline*. It should be water under the bridge. They are nice people and will be assets in running west coast operations," I stated.

"You actually don't need to convince me. They will be extremely valuable. They also seem rather excited about being part of *Jacqueline*. And, yes, they are both very nice," said Brandon.

"I think they realized that they seemed destined to remain in the number two spot, so now they get to be part of the number one fashion magazine," I commented.

"I guess the old adage of 'if you can't beat 'em, join 'em' rang true," agreed Brandon.

He took another bite of his dinner and savored the flavor in his mouth. Then he washed it down with some red wine. A nearly equal look of satisfaction came across his face. Then he spoke again.

"I've been doing a lot of thinking about what the *Adele* acquisition can mean for us. Not just the company, but us, personally. What would you think of moving our offices here to California? Most specifically, here to Santa Barbara?"

"Really? You are actually considering moving the company headquarters out of Manhattan?" I asked.

"We'd still have our Manhattan office and a lot of key staff would remain there. But there is a strong argument to be made that our biggest growth after the acquisition will be the entertainment fashion sector. Today's technology makes it possible for me to have my office pretty much anywhere," replied Brandon.

"Well, I love the idea. As much as I like Manhattan, I do miss Santa Barbara. Have you discussed this with your grandmother?"

Jacqueline Davenport was Brandon's maternal grandmother and the founder and President of Davenport Media and the namesake of its flagship entity, *Jacqueline* fashion magazine.

"I did raise the issue with her. She is on board as long as the company's involvement in the New York fashion industry and charitable events does not decline. I assured her that our presence in New York will be as strong as ever."

"What about your parents? I'm sure your mother isn't wild about the idea of you moving cross country," I said.

"No. But it's not like we all can't visit often. I mean, come on, they have a private jet at their use 24/7."

"Oh, and like you have ever flown commercial in your life," I teased.

"A few times in college, actually."

"Yeah, you have it rough. And I bet you flew first class."

"No comment," replied Brandon with a slight grin. "You know, if we do make the move, you could be more involved at the School of Arts."

I had graduated from the Davenport School of Arts at Santa Barbara University. I benefited greatly from the Davenport Scholarship fund and had volunteered on the fundraiser committee my senior year. I have donated faithfully to the fund since I started working, but I always wanted to be more involved.

"That would certainly be wonderful," I said.

We finished our dinner. The waiter cleared our dishes from the table. He then brought out a bottle of Francesca's finest champagne and two champagne flutes. He poured a sample in Brandon's glass. Brandon took a sip.

"Superb," Brandon remarked.

The waiter filled both of our glasses. He took our dessert order and then retreated to the kitchen.

"Okay, dinner is over. Per our agreement, no more discussion of business. The rest of the evening is just about us," Brandon said.

"I like focusing on us," I said.

"My favorite subject," said Brandon as he looked into my eyes. "Sip your champagne gently. You know how it can go to your head."

"So true," I said. I took a few sips of my champagne and giggled.

After a few more sips, I noticed something in the bottom of my glass. As Brandon saw me focusing on the object, he got up out of his chair and moved next to me. Then he bent down on one knee.

Chapter 3

"Ashley, the past four years have been the greatest of my life. And it is all because of you," said Brandon as he took my champagne glass and pulled out the beautiful diamond ring. He held my left hand and looked deeply into my eyes. My heart was racing with excitement.

"I know we had a few bumps along the way, but I hope that I have left no doubt about how much I love you. How much I cherish you. I want there to be no doubt that I want to spend the rest of my life with you. Ashley Sullivan, will you marry me?"

My hand was trembling and tears of joy were forming in my eyes. I was so overwhelmed that I could barely form the words in my mouth. But I didn't hesitate. I knew my answer. I had known how I would respond to this day for a long time.

"Yes," I replied. "Yes, I will marry you."

Brandon slid the ring onto my finger. We embraced and Brandon kissed me. His lips were warm and tender. The kiss was as passionate and sensual as any we had ever shared. But it was our first kiss an engaged couple.

"I love you," said Brandon.

"I love you, too," I replied.

I could hardly believe it. Four years ago Brandon Mitchell was an innocent crush. He was a distant fantasy. But that had all changed and now I was going to be his wife. I couldn't recall ever being so happy.

"Brandon, it is beautiful," I said as I looked down at the diamond engagement ring on my finger.

I never imagined that I would own such an exquisite piece of jewelry. But that really didn't matter to me. It was the symbol of our love that moved me.

"But you could have given me a ring out of a Cracker Jack box and I would have been happy."

"Really? I can take it back and run to the convenience store for some Cracker Jacks," joked Brandon.

"Well, let's not get too carried away," I said with a smile.

"You deserve the absolute best," said Brandon. "I had it especially designed for you. It is truly one of a kind, just like you."

The quartet had paused to give us a light round of applause at my agreement to marry Brandon. They resumed playing.

"May I have this dance, Miss Sullivan?" asked Brandon as he stood.

"Why, yes you may, Mr. Mitchell. However, I think we need to start thinking of me as the future Mrs. Brandon Mitchell."

"Ashley Mitchell has a nice ring to it," he said. "Or will it still be Ashley Sullivan? Or maybe Ashley Sullivan Mitchell?"

"Hmm, I haven't decided yet. But I like the sound of Mitchell being in the mix."

Brandon held me close as we danced in the moonlight. I rested my head against his chest. In that moment, I was comforted by the knowledge that I would be in Brandon's arms forever.

The waiter approached our table with our dessert. He caught sight of my engagement ring.

"Well, it looks as if congratulations are in order," he said with a smile.

Brandon and I paused from our dancing for a moment.

"Yes, thank you," I said.

"Perhaps you could wrap our dessert to go," said Brandon.

"Yes, sir," said the waiter.

Brandon and I resumed our dancing. We held each other close and danced until the waiter returned with our desserts in a small, discreet bag with the restaurant's logo. Brandon paid our check and left generous tips for the waiter and the string quartet. He then took me by the hand and led me back to our suite.

Chapter 4

"Hi, Ash," said Chelsea as she answered the phone.

Chelsea and I had been best friends and roommates since our freshman year in college. She had just graduated from Columbia Law School and was preparing to take the New York Bar Exam. She also planned on taking the California Bar Exam to keep open the possibility of practicing law and teaching courses at our alma mater, Santa Barbara University.

"Chels, you won't believe it!" I said. "Brandon and I are getting married!"

Chelsea screeched with delight and I had to hold the phone away from my ear. When she stopped, I put the phone back to my ear.

"Congratulations! I am so happy for you. How did he propose? When? Have you picked a date for the wedding? . . ."

"Chels, take a breath, sweetie," I said. I told her about Brandon's proposal the night before.

"We haven't picked a date for the wedding yet. I'd suspect at least several months from now, though."

"I can only imagine the type of wedding that comes with marrying Brandon Mitchell," said Chelsea.

"We haven't discussed any of that yet. I don't really want a big Manhattan or Hamptons wedding. If I can get away with it, I'd prefer something simpler and more intimate. As long as Brandon is the groom, my family is present, and you are my maid of honor, that is all I really need."

"Are you kidding me? Do you seriously think that you can marry Brandon Mitchell and not have it be one of the social events of the year?"

I thought about that for a moment. Chelsea had a point. But, I had simple tastes, and it was my wedding. That should count for something. But he was a Mitchell and Jacqueline Davenport was his grandmother. Realistically, a small ceremony was probably not possible.

"Well, I guess we will all need to compromise a little for the sake of family unity," I said. "We'll talk more when I get back home. I still need to call my parents."

"Okay. Tell them I said hi."

"I will. See you tomorrow."

I hung up with Chelsea and called my parents. They were, naturally, thrilled with the news. I was the oldest of two daughters and the first to get married. It took my mother about ten seconds to get into wedding planning mode.

I told them that Brandon and I would come for a visit soon. I told them hi for both Chelsea and Brandon. I told my mom that I would call her later in the week after I got back to New York.

"How did everyone take the news?" asked Brandon as he walked into the living room of our suite.

"Everyone is very excited. I think we will need to be very clear about what we want for our wedding or my mother will have everything coordinated with your mother by the end of the week," I said.

"I give them until the end of the day," said Brandon as he kissed me on the top of my head.

"You may be right about that," I said. "In all seriousness, though, we should start thinking about what we want. I could see this getting very much out of hand pretty quickly."

"Agreed. How about we start planning on the flight back to New York this afternoon?"

"Perfect. And we have to present a united front. Our mothers will run circles around us otherwise."

"Except we have a secret weapon," he said.

I looked up and raised an eyebrow.

"My grandmother," said Brandon. "She will be so thrilled that we are getting married that she will go along with convincing our mothers of just about anything we want."

I nodded my head in agreement with a conspiratorial smile. I had to admit that Jacqueline Davenport adored me. She saw me as the perfect woman for Brandon. I tended to agree with her – and so did Brandon.

Chapter 5

Brandon completed the paperwork for Davenport Media to purchase *Adele* fashion magazine. He informed the Davenport Board of Directors that it was now a done deal. They gave Brandon some half-hearted congratulations. Davenport's Board of Directors was not as enthusiastic about the acquisition as Brandon and Jacqueline were, but, in the end, they secured the necessary votes to move forward.

A number of decisions still needed to be made about the new Davenport Media west coast office. One of the most important decisions was moving the majority of the executive team from New York to California. Brandon and the executives of the former *Adele* agreed that the writers, photographers, and west coast editorial staff would remain in Los Angeles to actually cover the LA fashion and entertainment industries. The business operations would move to Santa Barbara to join Brandon and the *Jacqueline* executives who would be relocating from New York.

While there were still a number of details to work out, as soon as we were on board the company jet, Brandon turned his attention to a discussion about our future plans as a married couple. He seemed relaxed as he settled into his seat on the plane. He removed his jacket and tie. He unbuttoned his top shirt button and let out a sigh.

"I'm glad to have the acquisition finalized," he said.

"Me too. Now I can get your undivided attention," I said.

"I know that my parents will push for a grand wedding in either Manhattan or the Hamptons, but what do you want?" he asked me.

"All I want is to marry you. Where is less important. Nonetheless, I'd prefer a more intimate ceremony and reception."

"So, less than a thousand people," Brandon said with a smile.

"Don't even joke about that. I couldn't imagine a wedding that size. It's not like we are the future King and Queen of England or something."

"Yes. But my mother thinks that the Mitchell and Davenport names are every bit as important as the Windsors of England," said Brandon. "But I want this wedding to be what you want it to be. How have you always pictured your wedding day? I mean, doesn't every girl dream about her wedding day?"

"I guess most do. Honestly, I always pictured a rather simple ceremony with family and close friends and a reception where everyone would just have a great time. But I don't suppose your parents have ever been to a wedding reception where *YMCA* and the *Electric Slide* were played," I said.

"I don't suppose so," replied Brandon. "But I am sure that we can find a way to sneak those in. I bet my grandmother knows the *Electric Slide.* Probably *YMCA* too. Before we figure out where to hold the ceremony and reception, maybe we should decide when we would like to get married."

"What are you thinking?" I asked.

"As soon as possible. But seeing as how our families would never forgive us if we either eloped or had a quickie marriage at City Hall, we will have to allow enough time to plan."

"So, a Vegas wedding chapel is probably out of the question?" I teased.

"You may not care about the big society wedding, but I know that you are not walking down the aisle of a Vegas wedding chapel," said Brandon.

"How about a late autumn wedding? That would give us several months to plan. Once we settle on a place, we can book and get Save-the-Date cards out pretty quickly."

"Sounds perfect to me. We'll get some push back from my mother as she'll want at least a year to help plan a major wedding event, but we already know we are not going that route. So, a wedding toward the end of the year is certainly doable. Where would you like to get married?"

"How about Santa Barbara?" I asked.

Brandon thought for a moment. "That makes a lot of sense. My mother's side of the family is from there. We still have lots of relatives in the area. You have a lot of college friends still living in and around Santa Barbara . . ."

"It is where we met. It is where we first made love. It is where are going to settle down and raise a family," I added.

"Oh, yes. All of those things as well," said Brandon.

I playfully tapped him on the arm.

"I love the idea of getting married in Santa Barbara. I think that my grandmother will be thrilled with the idea. I bet my mother won't even be opposed, given all the family we have there. How will your parents feel about that?"

"I think they will be very happy with the choice. They assumed that I wouldn't be getting married in my hometown, so Santa Barbara makes as much sense as anywhere."

"Good. Then we at least have settled on that," said Brandon.

"Making good progress, I would say."

I pulled out my laptop, and we began searching possible wedding and ceremony venues. I'm not sure why we were even bothering. I think we both knew that the Lusso Resort & Spa was the perfect location. We could get married overlooking the Pacific Ocean and hold our reception in the grand ballroom at the resort. It was our special place and certainly ritzy enough to satisfy Brandon's mother.

That is what we finally decided. All that was left was checking possible dates. Of course we knew that Lusso would bend over backwards to accommodate us. Not being the height of the wedding season, there were available dates in October and November. We told them that we would get back to them as soon as we made a decision.

The jet touched down and taxied to a private hanger at Laguardia Airport. From there it was a short helicopter ride into the city. We went to Brandon's penthouse and showered and dressed for dinner at his parents' home that evening. Brandon hadn't yet informed anyone in his family about our engagement. He said that was the type of news that his family expected to receive in person over an elegant dinner.

The car picked us up at seven o'clock for the short ride to his parents.

"Nervous?" asked Brandon.

"A little. I hope they are happy about the news."

"Are you kidding? You know my family loves you. My grandmother has been rooting for us from the beginning. It nearly killed her when we broke up for that short time. They will all be very happy."

"Oh, don't forget to take off your ring until the announcement."

"What? Take off my ring?"

"If you walk in there with an engagement ring on, they will know right away. Trust me. My mother expects a grand announcement. Please. Just until after dinner. It doesn't change the fact that we are engaged."

It was the first time that I ever saw a look of fear in Brandon's eyes. It was clear that there was some sort of family protocol that he was expected to follow in this type of situation. I figured it was worth keeping the peace. I took off the ring and placed it in my purse.

"Thank you," said Brandon.

"You owe me. Big time," I replied.

"I will pay you back tonight," he said with a seductive look in his magnificent blue eyes.

Oh man. Those blue eyes of his got me every time. I melted inside.

"I look forward to it," I said as I took his hand in mine and gave him a kiss on the cheek.

Chapter 6

James and Patricia Mitchell lived in an elegant and large brownstone home. Whereas Brandon's penthouse was modern, his parents home was more classically decorated. We were seated in the formal dining room with its antique dining table and chairs. We were served our dinner on formal China dishes, used Sterling Silver utensils, and drank from crystal glasses.

While the setting was formal, it was by no means stuffy or pretentious. The Mitchells were friendly and genuinely warm people. I had grown quite fond of them over the four years that Brandon and I had dated. I liked them very much. Which was good, seeing as how they were going to be my in-laws.

James Mitchell was the former CEO of Davenport Media. He took an early retirement several years ago, and that was when Brandon took over as a 28-year-old CEO. Patricia Mitchell was Jacqueline Davenport's daughter and ran several important charities for the Davenport family.

Jacqueline Davenport and I had hit it off early in our relationship. She was an elegant, smart, and savvy woman. She had started *Jacqueline* fashion magazine and built a media empire. She still served as the President of Davenport Media and *Jacqueline* magazine.

We finished dinner and Brandon looked for his opportunity to announce the news of our engagement.

"With all of us gathered here this evening, Ashley and I have wonderful news to share."

The Mitchells and Jacqueline looked our way with anticipation. Brandon gave a broad smile and continued.

"Ashley and I getting married."

"Oh, what wonderful news," said Brandon's mother.

"Welcome to the family," Brandon's father said to me.

"I am so glad that you finally asked this lovely young woman to marry you," said Jacqueline. "I couldn't ask for a better granddaughter-in-law."

Patricia stood.

"Now, you two come here and give me a hug," she said with tears of joy in her eyes.

She embraced us both in a bear hug.

"I am so happy," said Patricia. "You know," she said to me, "For the longest time I thought that Brandon would never settle down. I had such high hopes when the two of you started dating. I couldn't ask for a better daughter-in-law. James and I love you both, so much."

I had tears in my eyes. I knew that Brandon's parents were fond of me, but I never expected such an outpouring of emotion from his mother.

"Where is the ring? Brandon, dear, you did get this lovely girl a nice ring, didn't you?"

"Yes, of course, mother."

I took the ring out of my purse and placed it back on my finger.

"Brandon wanted to surprise you with the news, so I took it off on the car ride over," I said.

"It is absolutely stunning. But you deserve no less," said Patricia.

"Thank you," I said, blushing.

"Now, sit down and tell me your thoughts about the wedding. Do you want to get married here in Manhattan or in the Hamptons?" asked Patricia.

"Patty, maybe Brandon and Ashley have other plans," said Jacqueline.

Brandon and I glanced at each other.

"Actually," Brandon said, "we have decided that the wedding will be in Santa Barbara."

Brandon and I detailed our reasons. We also explained how we planned to have the executive offices there. Surprisingly, we were met with no resistance. Brandon's family was so overjoyed at the mere fact that Brandon was getting married that they didn't want to throw up any roadblocks. Jacqueline and Patricia were even excited at the prospect of holding the wedding near to where so many of the Davenport family still lived.

After a wonderful evening with his family, Brandon and I returned to his penthouse. He made good on his promise and made passionate love to me. It had been a perfect ending to what had been an incredible twenty-four hours. After, I sat looking out over Central Park from Brandon's bedroom terrace.

I thought about the plans for our wedding. I pictured the type of home that we might purchase in Santa Barbara. I dreamed of the kids that we would have together. It was all coming true for me.

At that moment, I was blissfully unaware that Gina Arlotti would burst into our lives and change everything.

Chapter 7

Brandon and I had been engaged one week. We settled on the date for our wedding and made the reservation at Lusso. We were in Brandon's office going over the choices for our Save-the-Date notices.

"I like this one the best," I said.

"Looks great," Brandon replied.

"You really don't care which one we choose, do you?" I asked.

"It's not that I don't care . . ."

"That's all right. I didn't expect that you would have much an opinion on this sort of thing. Most guys don't."

Brandon smiled at me and gave me a gentle kiss on the lips.

"It's hard to think about invitation choices when you are standing in my office looking so amazing. Do you remember that night on my couch over there?"

"Brandon, we have too much to do to get me all turned on right now."

"Not even a quickie?"

"Not even a quickie. Nor heavy petting. Not even making out . . . at least not right now. Tonight you can have all of me for as long as you want," I said.

"Okay, I'm putting that in the bank," he said.

Brandon's phone on his desk buzzed. He hit the speaker button.

"Yes?" said Brandon.

Brandon's executive assistant's voice came over the speaker.

"Mr. Mitchell, a Ms. Gina Arlotti is in the lobby demanding to see you. Security told her that she would need to make an appointment, but she is very insistent that she is an old friend and that it is an emergency."

"Gina Arlotti? I don't know a . . . wait. Gina Arlotti the Italian model?" asked Brandon.

"I believe so, sir," replied Brandon's executive assistant.

"Tell her I can give her ten minutes. Send her up."

"Yes, Mr. Mitchell."

"Who is Gina Arlotti?" I asked.

"A model that I met in Italy about ten years ago. I barely remember the time we spent together."

"I see."

"I don't remember much about her. Let's just say that most of that particular trip to Italy was a blur. I was in my early 20s and partying pretty heavy that summer in Europe. I'm not proud of it, but there were many women that summer. Several were Italian models. And French and . . ."

"Okay. I get the picture," I interjected.

Brandon's playboy days had been infamous in the tabloids and pop culture news. It was part of his past that I had learned to accept. He slipped up once, and it nearly ruined us. But Brandon had changed.

"What do you think she wants?" I asked.

"I have no idea. I guess we will find out soon enough."

A few minutes later, Gina Arlotti stormed into Brandon's office. She was five feet ten inches and thin. She had a perfectly proportioned face that was absolutely gorgeous. Gina had beautiful curves and what appeared to be perfect breasts. Every inch of her let you know that she was a top super model. Or had been.

"Brandon, it has been a long time," said Gina.

"Yes, it has. Gina Arlotti, this is my fiancée, Ashley Sullivan. Ashley Sullivan, Gina Arlotti."

"Fiancée? Yes, I am aware of your recent engagement. I'm sad to say that this is going to make this all the more complicated for you," announced Gina.

"How so? Gina, I have to be honest, I barely remember our time together. I have absolutely no idea why you are even here," said Brandon.

"That doesn't surprise me in the least. I know that I was one of many women you entertained your summer in Europe. But I also know that you were the only man that I slept with that summer," replied Gina.

"I don't mean to be rude, but, exactly why should that be relevant to me?" asked Brandon.

"It is relevant because it leaves no doubt that you are the father of my ten-year-old son."

It felt like the oxygen had been sucked out of the room. Brandon and I stood there shocked at what we had just heard. Then Gina let the other shoe drop.

"As for your plans of marrying, that is something that we will need to discuss. Brandon is my husband."

"What?! Are you out of your mind?! . . ."

Gina held up her hand.

"Brandon, darling, don't. I know that we were so young and irresponsible, but we shared a night of passion that I will never forget. That night of passion produced a son. It also found us before a Justice of the Peace and married," she said.

"That was a mistake! One we both regretted and took care of the next day. How dare you come in here and make these wild accusations? What is it that you want? Money?" said Brandon.

"Brandon, dear. Are they really that wild of accusations? Think about it. You spent most of that trip drunk and fucking every pretty young model, actress, and socialite in Europe. I don't know, maybe you had a sense of romance the night we spent together. I do recall an annulment, but, as it turns out, that was not finalized," said Gina.

"What are you saying? I signed the paperwork. It was done before I left Italy," said Brandon.

"There is no official record of our annulment. Without that, we are legally married," replied Gina.

As I got over my initial shock I caught up with the actual conversation in the room. It finally registered that not only was Gina claiming that Brandon had a ten year old son, but that Brandon was married to Gina.

"What a minute," I said, "you were, or are, actually married to this woman?"

"Ashley, it was a drunken error in judgment. We had it annulled the next day. It's not like it was a real marriage," Brandon replied.

"Well, darling, a valid marriage certificate and no record of the annulment says it is a real marriage," said Gina.

"Stop calling me darling!" said Brandon.

"I can't believe this. I can't believe that you were married for even a night and didn't think to mention that to me once in four years!" I said.

"Ashley, please. It meant nothing. I hadn't given it any thought in over ten years. As for you, Gina, what do you want? Why are you coming and telling me this now?"

"I heard about your engagement on the news. It seemed only appropriate that you be made aware of the situation."

"Look, I will sign whatever I need to sign to get the marriage annulled or to divorce. Whatever it takes. And if the boy is my son, then I will make sure that he is taken care of. But you are not going to destroy my life. I am marrying Ashley."

"We shall see about that," said Gina coldly. "If you meet my terms, then, perhaps, I might see fit to end our marriage to allow you to marry Miss Sullivan. But my terms are not negotiable and they will cost you dearly. Whether enough of your life remains for Ashley to want to still marry you, well . . . I guess that remains to be seen. Of course, you could decide to see the silver lining in all of this and join the family that you didn't even know you had."

"I will provide for a son, but I am not going to be married to you. We are not, nor will we ever be, a family. And we will deal with why you didn't come to me sooner about all of this," stated Brandon.

"Brandon, darling, you are in no position to bluster. I hold all the cards here," replied Gina. She was cold as ice.

There had to be more to what was happening. There had to be a greater motive behind Gina's actions. And we still needed to find out of it was all true, but that would be easy enough. I had settled into the realization that it probably was true and that Gina was going to play hardball.

I gasped for breath and fought back tears. I felt like I had been punched in the gut by the shocking news that we had just received. It was going to shake the very foundation of the life Brandon and I were building together. In fact, it could quite possibly destroy any hopes we had of spending the rest of our lives together.

Gina Arlotti wanted more than to disrupt a wedding, she wanted to destroy Brandon's life. She wanted to deny me a life with him. Gina wanted to take everything we had for herself.

Chapter 8

I felt like I was in a bad dream. I stood beside the man I had promised to marry while another woman tried to destroy our future happiness.

Gina Arlotti was a woman from Brandon's past. Gina claimed that she and Brandon were legally married. She also claimed that Brandon had a ten-year-old son with her. Gina seemed hell bent on using the situation to gain more than what would be her fair share of support for their son. What most troubled me was that Gina seemed to be taking pleasure in the situation. As for me, I was still trying to catch my breath and gain some semblance of composure.

"I will have my lawyer contact you," Gina said to Brandon.

"Wait," replied Brandon. "What is his name? Assuming he is my son, I at least should know his name."

"Antonio," replied Gina. "Here." She handed Brandon a picture. "We'll be in touch."

With that, she turned and left Brandon's office. Brandon looked down at the picture and then he placed it on his desk.

I was still reeling from the news. Ten minutes before, we had been choosing our Save-the-Date stationary. I wish I had never heard of Gina Arlotti. But, if it were all true . . . I didn't know what we were going to do.

"Let me see," I said to Brandon as I held out my hand for the photograph.

He handed it to me. I looked at the face of a handsome boy that bore a definite resemblance to Brandon when he was a child. The picture, of course, was not definitive proof. But

I already had a sinking feeling about what the paternity test results would show.

"What are we going to do?" I asked as I wiped tears from my eyes.

"We will see what her lawyers have to say . . . what her demands are going to be. Then we will take it from there."

Brandon was shocked, to say the least, but he was calm. He had a steel look in his eyes. People didn't push Brandon around. If Antonio was his son then Brandon would, at the very least, make sure he was taken care of with the finest of everything. If Brandon and Gina's marriage had not been annulled, Brandon would fight to make sure that an annulment happened. None of that changed the fact that all of what I had learned was troubling.

"Why didn't you tell me?" I asked.

"About Antonio? I obviously didn't know. I may have been a playboy, but I would certainly make sure any child I had would be well provided for."

"I know that about you. That's not what I meant. Why didn't you tell me about the marriage?"

"Ashley, I already told you. I thought that it had been annulled the very next day. I really haven't thought about it since then."

"So it didn't cross your mind once in the past four years? You didn't think it might be worth mentioning when you were thinking of asking me to marry you?"

Brandon shook his head. "No. It didn't. I was drunk and foolish when it happened. It wasn't a real marriage in my mind. I never would have gone through with it if I hadn't been high as a kite. It meant nothing and was over within twenty-four hours."

"Seriously? How hard it would it have been to say 'Hey, Ashley, it was nothing, but once when I was drunk I got married for a day. I had it annulled . . . '"

"Ashley, please. Are we going to litigate this? I think we have bigger fish to fry at the moment."

Brandon was all business. You don't get to be an alpha billionaire without having a bit of an edge to you. I loved Brandon. He was kind and generous.

Brandon was the man of my dreams. But there was also no denying that he had that edge to him. When he was all about business, he could get an extreme tunnel vision that could make him insensitive to matters beyond what was directly in front of him.

"So my feelings don't matter?"

"Ashley, I didn't say that."

"You didn't have to," I said.

I started to cry again. I got up and stormed out of Brandon's office. Brandon let me go without protest. He knew it was futile to discuss it with me at that moment. We both needed more time to process the bombshell that Gina Arlotti had dropped on us.

I made a stop by the restroom and washed my face. I then headed to my office. I went in, closed my door, and drew the blinds to let my staff know that I did not want to be disturbed. I pulled out my cell phone and called my best friend Chelsea.

"I'm glad you called," said Chelsea as she answered. "Gives me an excuse to take a break from studying."

Chelsea had just graduated from Columbia Law School at Columbia University and was studying for the bar exam. Two bar exams, actually. The New York and California bar exams. Chelsea wanted to keep her options open based on the numerous job offers she had received.

Even though I knew that Chelsea was wearing her Columbia Law sweatshirt and sweatpants as she studied, she would still be the most stunningly beautiful woman I knew – super model gorgeous. She was also the smartest. Not only was she Valedictorian of our Santa Barbara University graduating class four years before, she was a top graduate in her law class at Columbia. More important than any of that, though, she had been my best friend since our Freshman year in college. Chelsea was always there for me.

"Chelsea, I don't know what I am going to do," I said through tears.

"Ash, sweetie, what is wrong?"

I told her the news. There was a stunned silence on the other end of the phone for a moment.

"Brandon has great lawyers. The best money can buy. They will find a way to settle this. I will help where I can as well. There is no way this Arlotti bitch is going to stop you from marrying Brandon."

"But what about the fact that Brandon never mentioned being married to her?"

"Does this raise trust issues? Like the time he cheated? Are you worried that there may be other things he may not be telling you?"

"Yes. Maybe. I don't know. What I do know is that he didn't tell me this. That bothers me enough."

"Ash, I'm not saying that it shouldn't, but I also wonder if it really wasn't that big a deal to Brandon. In his mind, it was nothing. I bet it didn't even register as something that he would need to mention. Men can be strange creatures."

"Do you think I'm overreacting?" I asked.

"I didn't say that. But it may not really be the issue that you think it is," said Chelsea.

"So, in other words, I may be overreacting?"

I could sense Chelsea grinning on the other end of the phone.

"Maybe we need to focus on the issue of whether Brandon is still legally married to Gina and how his having a son factors into your life," she answered. "How did you leave it with Brandon? Did you just storm out of his office in tears?"

Chelsea knew me too well. Sometimes I think that she knew me better than I knew myself.

"I probably need to go talk to him," I said. "I'll talk to you later. Now, you get back to your studying."

"Okay. Call me later when you know what your evening looks like."

"I will. Thanks, Chels."

"That's what a best friend is for," she said. "Talk to you later."

We hung up. I opened my office door and noticed my staff trying to look over without seeming obvious.

"I'm okay," I told them.

Chelsea helped me put things in perspective. I headed down the hall to Brandon's office. We would figure this out, together.

Chapter 9

"Ashley, I'm sorry," Brandon said, as soon as I stepped into his office.

"You're right. I should have mentioned my one night marriage to Gina. It meant nothing, but I should have told you, anyway. I don't want there to be anything between us. You are going to be my wife. Gina is not stopping our wedding."

"Thank you. I may have overreacted a bit. I just didn't want to think that you were keeping things from me. We had issues with trust four years ago. That's behind us now, but I need to know that the honesty and trust we have built is genuine."

Brandon put his arms around me and held me close.

"It absolutely is. Ashley, I love you more than life itself. I will fix this. I promise. We will be married this year. On the date we chose. Gina doesn't know who she is taking on."

"So no other quickie marriages I should know about?" I asked, trying to lighten the mood.

"None. I swear."

"Brandon, I'm afraid. What are we going to do? I mean, Gina must be telling the truth. I don't why she would come here and make accusations she couldn't back up. Especially if she is getting lawyers involved."

"Because lawyers are the most honest and trustworthy people in the world?"

"They at least need to operate within the confines of the legal system. You are either legally married or you are not."

"True. But I'm sure there is more than one way to legally go about this. I've already spoken to my lawyers and they are investigating options as we speak. Even if the marriage is still valid, we will get it annulled quickly," remarked Brandon.

"What about Antonio?" I asked.

"That will be more complicated. If he is my son . . ."

"If? You did see the same photo I did, right?"

"Granted, he looks a lot like me at his age. But I still want hard evidence. We will get the paternity test done ASAP. I will provide for him, but there are bigger questions . . ."

"Like if he will be a part of our lives?"

"Yes. I don't know what Gina will demand or what we can do about visitation rights or any sort of custody. My lawyers will provide options. But how do you feel about it?"

"If he is your son, and let's assume that he is, I think you should be a part of his life. I think we should be a part of his life. Brandon, you can't just send checks and establish a trust fund for the boy. He needs to know his father and you need to know him."

"Yes. I would want to be part of his life. I know we discussed having kids, and this wouldn't change that, but it would mean that there is already a ten-year-old boy who would be part of our lives in some way."

"We will figure it out. Antonio's well being has to be a priority. I guess we need to see how difficult and demanding Gina is going to be about all of this. I got the impression that she wants to extract more than a pound of our flesh in this process."

"Hmm. I think you might be right," said Brandon. "But we will figure this out. Besides, we can always resort to locking her in a room with Chelsea and see who comes out alive."

"Gina seems like a tough bitch, but my money would be on Chelsea," I said with a grin. This was the first time that I could even think about a smile since Gina Arlotti stormed onto the scene.

Brandon's desk phone buzzed.

"Mr. Mitchell, your lawyer is on line two," said Teresa, Brandon's executive assistant.

"Thank you," said Brandon. He picked up the phone and pressed line two. "Andrew, I have Ashley with me, I'm putting you on speaker phone."

Brandon pushed another button and then placed the phone back in its cradle.

"So, what do you have for us?" asked Brandon.

"Several things. We should set up a face to face as soon as possible, but I can give you an overview of where we are at currently," said Andrew through the speaker on the phone.

"Okay, let's have it," replied Brandon.

"Well, the paternity test is very simple. A cheek swab, known as a buccal swab, from you, the boy, and his mother. They can run a genetics test on the DNA and determine whether you are the boy's father with over ninety-nine percent accuracy. The test results can be completed within a matter of days."

"Okay. What about financial support and visitation or joint custody?" Brandon asked.

"We will need to see what Ms. Arlotti is demanding and take it from there. There will be a minimum in child support that you would need to provide, but given your vast resources . . ."

"Andrew, the issue is not the money. I'm not going to fight supporting Antonio. I will provide him with the best of everything. That is not in question. I do, however, want to limit what Gina can claim for herself," Brandon interjected.

"That will be tougher if it turns out that you have been legally married for the past ten years. She could demand a lot of money to agree to an annulment. If you need to file for divorce, she could make it ugly and expensive," replied Andrew.

"Well, we will fight her on that. She is not going to extort money out of me for a marriage that was a drunken mistake and, I assumed, was annulled a day later. The only reason it wouldn't actually have been annulled is if she did something to prevent it being finalized," barked Brandon into the speaker phone.

"That could be hard to prove," said Andrew.

"Hard or not, she isn't getting a penny out of me for herself. I'll give the world to Antonio, but I don't owe Gina anything."

"Understood. I expect to speak with her attorneys this afternoon. I will know more after that. Brandon, this could be a bit dicey. We are not just dealing with the U.S. Court system. You were married in Italy. Gina and Antonio are Italian citizens. International cases are always more complicated. Nonetheless, our office in Rome will be a real asset."

"That is why I pay you such a handsome retainer. Get this done. I have a wedding to plan with the woman that I actually want to marry."

"We will do everything we can as quickly as possible," said Andrew. "I will call you this evening after I speak with Ms. Arlotti's attorneys."

"Fine. Call me on my cell," replied Brandon.

"Okay. Talk to you later."

Brandon ended the call and let out a deep sigh. "Let's call it a day and get a drink," he said.

I wasn't a big drinker. In fact, a few glasses of wine and I was pretty much done for. I especially didn't drink before noon but, after the morning we had, I was ready to knock a drink back.

"I guess it's five o'clock somewhere," I said.

"Indeed," replied Brandon.

We left his office and Brandon instructed Teresa that he would be out of the office for the rest of the day. He put his arm around me and we headed for the elevator. We had a challenging situation, but I was comforted by Brandon's touch.

I loved Brandon and longed for him as much as the day we met. I couldn't help but feel the jolt of electricity that coursed through my body when he touched me. I hoped that sensation would never go away.

Chapter 10

Brandon and I sat in the Ty Bar of the Four Seasons hotel in Manhattan. The Ty Bar had been recently renovated and anchored the grand 57th Street lobby of the hotel. Brandon was drinking a custom barrel bourbon made exclusively for Ty Bar. I sipped a Black Cherry Collins.

Brandon stared in silence at the photo of Antonio. He was deep in thought. He had the same look on his face that he got when he was considering a major business decision.

No doubt that Brandon was thinking about what it was going to be like to be a father to Antonio and how it would change our lives. There was still the paternity test, but we had little doubt as to the outcome. The picture of Antonio looked like it had been lifted from James and Patricia Mitchell's mantle, where they displayed photos of Brandon as a child.

"He's a good-looking boy," I said after a few minutes.

"I still can't believe that he is ten years old, and this is the first I am learning about him," said Brandon.

"Why would Gina wait so long to tell me? Why, if we are, as she claims, still legally married, did she not come to me sooner? Even if all she wanted was money, and I'm sure that is what this is mostly about, why now?"

"I know. It doesn't make much sense. It's not like you recently came into your fortune. But I suspect that it is more than money. In fact, I'm not so sure money is the motivating factor," I said.

"How so?" asked Brandon.

"Think about it. If it were primarily about money, Gina would have come to you years ago. Probably as soon as she knew she was pregnant with your child. Especially if she knew that the annulment of your marriage was never finalized."

"That certainly makes sense. So what is her motivation?"

"I wish I knew. I suppose we will learn more after Andrew speaks with her lawyers. But I get the feeling that her story doesn't fully add up. Call it woman's intuition."

"So you think she is making it all up?"

"No. That wouldn't make much sense. It's too easy to disprove paternity and the legality of your marriage for her to do that. Within a matter of days, we will know for certain about both. Besides, unless she has access to your childhood photos or somehow got very creative on Photoshop, Antonio's picture is pretty convincing."

"Ashley, you know that I pride myself on staying at least one step ahead of the competition and anticipating what is going to happen. But I am completely at a loss here. Beyond accepting that the annulment never happened, and that Antonio is my son, I don't know what to think about all of this."

"Would it be so crazy to suggest that Gina wants what we have? That she wants the life that we are building together?" I offered it more as a suggestion than a question.

"Nothing is probably too crazy to consider," Brandon replied. He finished his Bourbon and motioned for the waiter.

"Another, please," Brandon instructed the waiter when he arrived at our table.

"Yes, sir. For you, miss?" asked the waiter.

"No, thank you. One will be enough for me," I replied.

I was content to nurse my Black Cherry Collins. As it was, I would feel a slight buzz by the time I finished the one drink. Ashley Sullivan, lightweight.

"Ashley, you are amazing. I know how hard all of this is on you. Just a few hours ago we were planning our wedding. Now . . ."

"Brandon, don't. I love you. Yes, I was shocked and upset by all of this. But I am glad that we know about Antonio. We need to make sure he is provided for. I wonder why Gina waited so long. I worry that she will be extremely disruptive in putting us through this."

I rested my hand on top of Brandon's.

"Andrew and his legal team are top notch and will figure out our best option. When I agreed to marry you, I knew that meant for better or for worse. I guess we are getting the worse up front."

"Yes, but we aren't even married yet."

"That doesn't matter. Look how far we have come. Four years ago, I could not have imagined having the life that I have and being engaged to you. We'll get through this," I said.

"Besides, none of that changes the fact that, most likely, you have a son. We need to be thinking about how we can have a positive role in his life."

The waiter returned with Brandon's bourbon. Brandon took a sip. He let it slide down his throat.

"I do want to be part of his life. I want us to be part of it. You will make a great mother to our children and a great step mother to Antonio. I only hope that I can be half as good at being a father."

"You will be a great dad. I wouldn't have agreed to marry you if I didn't know what an amazing father you would be."

"I don't know what Gina will demand or what the lawyers can work out, but what should we be fighting for here? What will be best for Antonio?" asked Brandon.

"See, the fact that you asked that question proves that you have it in you to be a great dad," I replied.

"I don't know what the laws are regarding our particular situation. I especially don't know how Antonio being an Italian citizen plays into this, but I think we should be as large a part of his life as we can. I think we fight to be active in his life beyond just visitation rights. Some sort of custody, even if it's only summers and vacations."

Brandon gazed admiringly into my eyes.

"Have I told you that you are amazing?"

"Yes. But there's nothing amazing about doing what is best for Antonio. If we are going to be married, then Antonio is going to be my stepson. We will be the best family we can be. No matter what we have to do to make it work."

Brandon's cellphone rang.

"It's Andrew," he said as he glanced down at his screen.

"Andrew, what do you have for us?"

Brandon listened for a moment as Andrew spoke.

"Okay, we will see you then," said Brandon when Andrew finished speaking. He hung up and looked at me.

"We have a meeting set for tomorrow afternoon at Andrew's office. Gina and her lawyer will be there to negotiate some sort of settlement. Well, Gina said to meet her demands, but her lawyer seemed more ready to talk. Gina and I will also provide the mouth swabs for the paternity test. Andrew wants to meet with us later this afternoon to go over our strategy."

"What time?" I asked.

"Three o'clock."

"Okay. Will Antonio be there tomorrow?" I asked.

"I don't think so. Andrew indicated that he is in New York with Gina, but will be looked after by a nanny. I guess part of what we will negotiate is our being able to see him during their time in New York. We will just have to wait until tomorrow to see how this all begins to work out."

I took a deep breath. I felt anxious. I hoped that an agreement would be reached the next day. Somehow, I felt that it would not be so easy. Call it my woman's intuition again, but Gina had claws and she wasn't afraid to use them.

Chapter 11

Despite the day that we had, Brandon needed to get some work done that evening. He was reviewing some documents in the study at the penthouse. I had moved in the year earlier. I invited Chelsea over for dinner and we had ordered from Ming's, our favorite Chinese restaurant in New York.

"I just love their Sesame Chicken," Chelsea said.

"And the egg rolls," I added.

"And the fried rice," said Chelsea.

"We could do this all night. We basically love everything from Ming's."

"Agreed," Chelsea said as she popped an egg roll in her mouth.

It was wonderful spending some quality time with my best friend. It had been a trying day and time with Chelsea always made lightened my mood. She would also be able to offer great insight. Chelsea had just graduated from Columbia Law School. Beyond that, she was easily the smartest person I knew.

"So, what do you think?" I asked her.

"Well, I am not a lawyer yet . . ."

"Oh, just that pesky bar exam to get out of the way," I said. "A mere formality."

"Easy for you to say. You're not the one taking it."

"Oh, come on. You are going to ace that thing. Then you are going to ace the California Bar Exam so you can take a job at a law firm in Santa Barbara." I smiled at her.

Chelsea and I met as freshman roommates at Santa Barbara University. We have been best friends ever since. I very much wanted her to take a position back on the west coast so we could be close by. I couldn't imagine not having Chelsea in the same city.

"We shall see," she said. "There is one law firm that is very attractive. Plus, Santa Barbara University would love to have me teach some classes. I think that would be a lot of fun."

"Not to mention you would be near your best friend," I added.

"That would be the best reason of all. But, we can talk about all of that later. I know you want my opinion on this case, let's focus."

"Right. Sorry, Chels. I guess I am just really nervous about what might happen tomorrow at the meeting."

"Classic avoidance," noted Chelsea. "You can be a master at it."

"Good thing I have you around," I said.

"Here is what I think," Chelsea continued. "I'm sure that Andrew Bennett went over all of this with you guys, but the offer that Brandon is willing to make for child support is better than anything a court would award in the United States. Even with Brandon's wealth. I'm not sure about the courts in Italy, but I can't imagine they would award more either."

"Andrew's firm has an office in Rome," I said, "that is what they told us."

"I don't think the child support will be the issue. What you have to worry about is Gina granting an annulment," Chelsea said.

"That's what I'm afraid of. That woman is cold. I get very bad vibes from her."

"The good news," said Chelsea, "is that she can make it difficult . . ."

"How is that good news?" I asked.

"Let me finish. She can make it difficult, but I don't think she has much ground to stand on. I actually think that the law is on Brandon's side. I believe there is even legal precedence in Italy on annulments when intent to have a real marriage is not there."

"Come again," I said.

"If two people get married as a joke, on a dare, if one of the parties wanted an open marriage. That sort of thing."

"So, two people getting married while drunk and then agreeing the very next day that it was a mistake . . ."

"I'm pretty confident that would qualify," said Chelsea.

"Okay, I understand all of that. So why do I feel so nervous about this? Why does Gina have me so rattled?"

"Because this is emotional. You and Brandon have had a lot dumped on you. And, quite frankly, you are dealing with a woman who seems highly motivated and, just a tad, irrational."

"That's the weirdest part. Why Gina waited ten years. She knew Brandon was a billionaire ten years ago," I said.

"Hard to say. Probably had enough money back then. Had a great life. Why complicate it by letting Brandon know they had a son together. Assuming, of course, that he is actually the father."

"I saw the picture. Pretty convincing on its own."

"Also, even if Gina is a bit nuts, it would be easy to prove her claims false. Not likely she would fly to New York from Italy to lie about all of this."

"But you think we have reason to be optimistic?" I asked.

"Again, I am not a lawyer yet. And, even if I where, I'm not handling the case, so I don't have all the details. But, based on what I do know, I think there is reason to be cautiously optimistic. Ash, I do want you to remember that anything can happen. You need to be prepared for things to go sideways. If Gina is really intent on playing hardball she can make life very difficult. Even if you eventually get the best possible outcome."

"I know. I do feel better having you look at this and talking through it with me."

"Hey, what are best friends for? And, you know, whatever happens, I am always here for you."

"I know that too," I said.

Chelsea and I hugged. She was truly the most amazing BFF. More than a friend, she was like a sister to me.

"Ash, this is going to all work out. Andrew Bennett is an amazing attorney. Brandon is smart and resourceful, in the best way, and, at some point, common sense and reasonableness will play a factor."

"Thanks," I said.

I hoped that Chelsea was right. She usually was, but she hadn't met Gina. Most people didn't mess with Chelsea, but I think Gina would be one of those people who would relish taking her on. Gina was cold and wanted Brandon and I to be miserable. That worried me.

Chapter 12

Bennett, Sanders, & Ross was one of the largest and most accomplished legal firms in the country. Andrew Bennett had been Brandon's attorney for over a decade. I had no idea what Brandon paid the firm in a legal retainer, but I knew that it was a hefty sum of money. According to Brandon, they were worth every penny.

We sat in one of the conference rooms down the hall from Andrew Bennett's office. They occupied several floors of a mid-town Manhattan high rise and the conference room had a spectacular view of the New York skyline. The entire firm had plush carpeting that was well above your typical office grade. The tables and desk were a rich mahogany, and the seating was deep leather.

"So how much are you paying them?" I whispered into Brandon's ear as we took our seats at the large conference table.

"Let's just say that I have paid for at least a few floors of their space in the building. But Andrew is . . ."

"I know. Worth every penny."

"Brandon, Ashley, it is good to see you," said Andrew as he entered the conference room. He dropped a large folder onto the table and shook our hands.

Andrew Bennett was in his early sixties, but looked at least ten years younger. He was nearly six feet tall and thin. He had light brown hair with just a hint of gray and a warm smile. He wore a finely tailored, charcoal suit from Brooks Brothers and a dark blue striped tie. It was a "power suit" that showed he meant business.

Similar to Brandon, Andrew had an air of supreme confidence. Not cockiness or arrogance, but confidence that he knew what he was doing and would succeed. Of course, he had a forty-year track record that supported his case.

"Here's the deal," Andrew said as he sat down. "Ms. Arlotti and her attorney will be here in a few minutes. A technician from a DNA testing lab will be in at the same time to collect the buccal swabs from you and Ms. Arlotti. We are assuming, and I don't think you disagree, that the test is more of a formality. We just need to establish beyond doubt the fact that you are Antonio's father. Our discussions today are operating under the assumption that paternity will be confirmed."

"Yes. That is what we assume," said Brandon.

"Based on what we discussed last night, we will demand proof that your marriage to Ms. Arlotti was not annulled as you believed. We will push for an annulment. We will offer full financial support for Antonio and request joint custody be implemented after a period of you getting to know Antonio. We will not agree to pay any alimony to Ms. Arlotti, given that neither of you ever intended for this to be a real marriage. As I mentioned last night, there is precedent in the Italian courts for this argument. Any questions?"

"No. I'm counting on you to make this happen," Brandon replied.

"That's what I am here for," said Andrew. "Look, I know I said that this would be tricky, and Ms. Arlotti wants to play hardball, but I was encouraged by what our Rome office told us about some recent cases in Italy that are both reasonable and in our favor."

"I hope you are right," I commented.

Andrew smiled a broad smile.

"I never make a move without all the facts," he said. "We are in a good position. Ms. Arlotti is tough, but her lawyers know what we know. Unless she is willing to perjure herself, there is no defense against annulment. Even if she did, it is her word against Brandon's. As far as Antonio is concerned, once we verify paternity, he will have dual citizenship in Italy and the United States. It gives a stronger case for some measure of joint custody."

A young woman entered the conference room.

"Mr. Bennett, Ms. Arlotti, and Ms. Shay are here," said the young woman.

"Thank you, Stephanie. Has the technician from the lab arrived?" said Andrew.

"Not yet, sir."

"Tell Ms. Arlotti and Ms. Shay that we will be with them in a few minutes. I want to begin with the buccal swab test, so we will wait until the lab representative arrives."

"Yes, sir." Stephanie turned and exited the conference room.

"Is Gina's attorney Barbara Shay?" asked Brandon.

"Yes. She's a partner in Hanson, Bloomfield, and Shay," replied Andrew. "You know her?"

"No. Just of her. She can be a real pit bull," said Brandon.

"Perfect for Gina," I said.

"Barbara can be a pit bull, but she is clear about the facts. As long as Ms. Arlotti accepts her counsel, we are fine," said Andrew.

"If Gina doesn't?" I asked.

"We'll still be fine. It will just take longer and be more of a headache."

Stephanie poked her head into the conference room.

"The lab technician just arrived," she announced.

"Thank you," said Andrew. "Please show everyone back."

Stephanie nodded her head and closed the door. She headed down the hall toward the floor's reception area. A minute later, she was back with Gina Arlotti, Barbara Shay, and the lab technician. She showed them into the conference room. Andrew greeted them. Both Gina and Barbara sat across from us at the table.

Andrew introduced the lab technician. He opened a small case and took out two cotton, swab-like sticks and two containers. One was marked with Gina's name and the other with Brandon's. There was a place for the technician to write the date and time that he collected the DNA samples.

He swabbed the inside of Gina's cheek, placed it her container, and sealed it. He then did the same with Brandon. He noted the time and filled that in on each container.

"That's it," he announced. He placed the containers back into his case and shut it.

"We will have the results in a couple of days," said the technician. With that, he exited the conference room.

Gina's eyes bore into Brandon. She appeared as cold as ever, but something about her stare told me that she did not like the counsel she had received from her attorney. I hoped that meant that Andrew was correct about the case being in our favor. Could this all be settled so we could get on with our lives? I took a deep breath as Barbara Shay began to speak.

Chapter 13

"It is my understanding that we are in agreement on the likely results of the paternity test," said Barbara Shay. "For that reason, I propose that we begin with the issue of child support for Antonio Arlotti. With the provision, naturally, that it is based on the paternity of Mr. Mitchell being confirmed."

"My client is in agreement with that," said Andrew.

"Fine," said Barbara. "My client is seeking child support that will provide for Antonio's care in a manner that is in keeping with Mr. Mitchell's resources. My client also seeks back-payment for support that would have been received for the past ten years."

"Mr. Mitchell is prepared to pay a generous amount in child support for Antonio's ongoing care," said Andrew.

He handed a document to Barbara Shay, and she looked it over.

"As you can see, it far exceeds any amount that you are likely to secure for your client from the courts, either in the United States or Italy," commented Andrew.

He paused a moment to allow Barbara Shay and Gina Arlotti to reflect on what he had just said.

I had no legal background, but when I told Chelsea what Brandon wanted to offer in child support, she had nearly fallen out of her chair. Andrew's statement was not some attorney tactic. Nor was it an exaggeration. Chelsea had told me, that even with Brandon's vast wealth, no court would award as much as he offered on his own.

Gina had to be more than satisfied with the offer, but she sure didn't show it. She had a poker face. Barbara Shay had her lawyer face on, but she knew that Andrew was right. Besides, Brandon had stated all along that Antonio would get the best of everything. And he meant it.

"My client would also like to establish a trust fund for Antonio, which may be accessed to pay for his college education. There will be restrictions on the amount that may be withdrawn from the fund in any given year, but it will be sufficient for Antonio to attend any college of his choice, plus provide living expenses while in school," said Andrew.

"That, too, goes beyond what would be required of my client if we were to go to court to settle this matter."

Andrew was good. I understood why Brandon was willing to pay so much to retain his firm as his legal counsel. Barbara Shay was actually speechless.

She and Gina Arlotti continued to look at the document that outlined Brandon's child support offer. After a few more moments, they whispered to each other. Barbara nodded her head when they were finished.

"This offer is acceptable to my client. Nonetheless, it fails to address the back-payment of support for the past ten years. Ms. Arlotti has born the entire expense of raising Antonio up until this point. It seems only fair that she be reimbursed for those expenses," said Barbara.

"I'm afraid that is unacceptable," said Andrew. "Mr. Mitchell was unaware that he possibly had a son until yesterday morning. Ms. Arlotti made no attempt to contact Mr. Mitchell at any point these past ten years. My client has no responsibility for back payments. It is unreasonable to be considered delinquent on support that he had no way of knowing may be needed."

"He got me pregnant and you want to tell me that he has no responsibility for our son?!" shouted Gina.

"Ms. Arlotti, Mr. Mitchell is taking more than full responsibility for the care of your son," replied Andrew. "But to expect him to reimburse you when you made no attempt to inform him that he had fathered a child –"

"Outrageous! How do you know that I did not contact Brandon? He simply ignored me."

"Gina, please. Let me do the talking," pleaded Barbara.

"Ms. Arlotti, Brandon Mitchell is a high profile individual. He is now and was ten years ago. It would have been very easy for you to have contacted Davenport Media and gotten a message of that importance to him," said Andrew.

"But if you would rather take chances with the courts . . ." Andrew rested his hands on the table.

"Please, give us a moment," said Barbara almost apologetically. She whispered in Gina's ear.

I was sure that they were not sweet nothings. Barbara had to know that if it went to court that they would be awarded less than the offer on the table. That even included the potential of winning back ten years of back payments.

Brandon, Andrew, and I exchanged glances. I think we were all confident that Barbara would convince Gina to accept the child support offer and drop any demand of back payments. To be honest, Brandon would make back payments if it would miraculously improve Antonio's past. But that wasn't possible. He had no desire to reward Gina for keeping the news of a son secret for ten years.

When Gina and Barbara were finished speaking, Barbara looked back at us from across the table.

"My client will accept the child support offer as presented, with no additional stipulations," said Barbara.

"Excellent. Now, shall we move on to discuss the matter of custody?" asked Andrew.

"Yes," said Barbara.

"Hold it just a minute," interrupted Gina. "I have no intention of discussing custody before we settle the matter of our marriage. Antonio's care is secure. What about mine? I want to discuss alimony."

"Are you nuts?" said Brandon. "We never had a real marriage. My understanding was that we had annulled the marriage the day after we foolishly married in our drunken state. There is nothing between us, Gina. There never was."

"Except for a night in Milan. The one where you married me and got me pregnant."

"I don't what sort of game you are playing, Gina. I have no idea why you waited ten years to bring any of this to my attention. I'm actually pissed that you withheld the fact that I have a son. A son whom I could have been providing for and been a father to for the past ten years. But none of that changes the fact that we never intended to be married. I don't owe you anything."

"Enough. Neither one of you say anything else," interjected Andrew. "Ms. Shay and I can handle this."

Gina ignored Andrew.

"A marriage certificate states that we were married. The absence of an annulment record means that we have been married for ten years and are married today. If you want to end the marriage, then I want alimony," said Gina coldly. There was no emotion in her voice. It was all very matter of fact.

"Besides," she continued, "what about Antonio? We wouldn't want him to be some bastard child. I will not have him carry the stigma of being born out of wedlock. Because that is what annulment would be. It would say we were never married."

"Really? . . ." began Brandon.

"Brandon, I think it best . . ." interjected Andrew.

"No," replied Brandon. "I am going to say this."

Andrew threw up his hands.

"Gina, you and I both know that your desire to push for a divorce over an annulment has nothing to do with your concern about Antonio being stigmatized. I don't even think that it carries the stigma that it used to. There are a lot of children who are born to parents who are not married," said Brandon.

"This is about money. This is about you trying to get your hands on my money. Why the hell do you think you deserve it?"

"Because we are married. The price of getting out of this marriage is a guarantee from you of my alimony payments," replied Gina evenly.

"But we never meant to really get married. We were drunk. We wouldn't have gone through with it otherwise. When we sobered up, we signed annulment papers the next day. It was over and done with it. At least it should have been," said Brandon.

I think that Andrew had enough. He wanted to maintain control over the situation and probably felt that it was going to spin out of control.

"Perhaps we should take a break," offered Andrew. "Barbara, you and miss Arlotti are free to use the conference room. We will go down the hall to my office."

"Yes, thank you," replied Barbara.

Brandon, Andrew, and I got up from the table and exited the conference room. Gina just looked down at the conference room table. She was seething with anger.

Chapter 14

"What just happened in there?" asked Brandon once we were in Andrew's office.

"Everything was moving along fine, and then . . ."

"Well, it is clearly about alimony," said Andrew. "If the marriage is annulled, that ends all discussion of Ms. Arlotti receiving alimony. Legally, the marriage would never have happened. It doesn't change paternity obligations for child support, but it would leave no room to negotiate alimony."

"I don't understand how Gina could make a valid claim to alimony even if we divorced. It wasn't really a marriage. Legally, yes, I suppose, but . . ." said Brandon.

"And there is the rub," said Andrew. "Legally, it is a marriage. That opens a claim, no matter how weak, to alimony. If Gina fights us on that, it could delay your wedding. It could also complicate moving forward on a discussion of custody."

"Shit. So she is playing us?" said Andrew.

Andrew simply shrugged his shoulders.

"What could she get if alimony were to be paid?" I asked out of curiosity.

"No way. She isn't getting a dime out of me for herself," replied Brandon.

"With what Brandon is worth? Many millions of dollars," answered Andrew.

"Ashley, we can't even consider that. It's a joke of a marriage. On principle, I don't want a record of ten years of marriage to Gina Arlotti."

"And what about Antonio? Are you okay with him officially being born out of wedlock?" I asked.

"It's not really a stigma anymore, Ashley. Besides, none of that changes the fact that Gina is his mother, I am most likely his father, and his mother and father never loved each other. Married or not, Gina and I never had any feelings for each other. It was the mistake of a misguided twenty-two-year-old," said Brandon.

"I wouldn't discuss it that way with him," I offered.

"Of course not. But you get my point," said Brandon.

"I get that you don't want to pay alimony. Nor should you have to pay under the circumstances. But what about getting on with our lives? Gina can make life very difficult for us. And we don't want an even harder fight over joint custody of Antonio," I said.

"If Brandon only wants annulment and Gina refuses, we are at a stalemate. We try to negotiate. We hope that we can convince her to accept terms for an annulment," said Andrew.

"Andrew, the amount of child support that I have offered will cover a very nice home and everything else for Antonio. Gina still benefits. She will be able to live large as long as she has at least partial custody of him," said Brandon.

"Until Antonio becomes an adult. Then child support stops. Brandon, Gina may be playing a longer game here. Maybe she has fallen on hard times. Who knows? But she waited ten years to raise this as an issue," said Andrew.

Brandon let out a sigh. "We should press her on that."

I put my arm around him and hugged him. He was tense.

"We can. But, to be honest, I'm not sure what difference it makes from a legal perspective. We negotiate annulment or divorce or fight it out in court," said Andrew.

"There has to be a way to get the annulment," said Brandon.

"We could threaten to retract the child support offer and have everything go to court. Barbara may then convince Gina that she will end up with a lot less in child support that way. Gina may reconsider alimony," said Andrew.

"We could. But I want Antonio to have what I have offered. It would be an empty threat. I don't want to bluff here," replied Brandon.

"I'm also concerned that Gina is more concerned about what she gets out of this more than Antonio's child support," I stated.

"Your woman's intuition?" asked Brandon.

"Yes, I guess. But think about it. Gina waits ten years to show up and announce that you are legally married and have a ten-year-old son together. I know that it may not have any legal baring, but it does mean something. Andrew may have been on to something."

"What was that?" asked Andrew.

"When you commented that maybe she has hit on hard times recently," I said. "Do we have any idea of how her modeling career is going? What sort of debt she may have?"

"That would explain things. If she had plenty of money, she may not have had any interest in bringing Brandon into her life . . ." said Andrew.

"Then her modeling career comes to end, she is living beyond her means, and suddenly the bank of Brandon is looking pretty good," concluded Brandon.

"Of course, this is all speculation," said Andrew.

"But a good theory. One that probably makes the most sense," replied Brandon.

"I agree," said Andrew, "but while it may explain motive, it doesn't provide a legal solution. Brandon, I need to know what you want to do. As we have discussed, there is clear precedence in the Italian courts for an annulment. The question is how hard you want to press for it?"

"I don't want this getting tied up in court. I won't make Ashley put our wedding on hold. And I certainly don't want to jeopardize custody negotiations. But I want the annulment."

"Brandon, I get that you never really meant for this marriage to happen. I understand you wanting to erase it from your history, but maybe it is easier to just file for divorce and agree to some form of alimony. I know that means Gina, in a sense, wins, but we can get on with our lives. We have to ask what that is worth," I said.

Brandon rubbed his hand across his face. He thought about what I had said. He let out a sigh.

"But that means that you would be marrying a divorced man. It means that the entire time that we have been together that I was married to someone else," Brandon replied.

"Technically, yes. But only in a legal sense. And neither one of us knew that a legal marriage even existed. Do you understand what I am trying to say?"

"Yes. But it would bother me writing an alimony check to her. An alimony she doesn't deserve."

"So don't write the check. Set up an account and let your accountant handle it. Brandon, sweetheart, would you honestly even notice the money wasn't there?"

"Yes. But I get the point you are making. On principle, I don't want to do it. But the money wouldn't change our lifestyle any. It would allow us to just move on from all of this."

"Or, here's a thought. Why don't you set up a job for her at the magazine? She is, or was, a fashion model. Surely she could make some contribution," I suggested.

"I don't think she wants to work for me," said Brandon.

"It's a big company. It's not like you would ever see each other. With direct deposit, she wouldn't even have to see your name on any paycheck. If its financial security she is looking for . . ."

"Ashley may be on to something," offered Andrew. "We could structure a simple contract that provides her with job security, sort of like tenure for college professors. The only problem is that she may have in her head that she is owed alimony and shouldn't have to accept a job. But, it may be worth a shot. I think I can make the case that we can offer an outcome better than she will get in court."

Brandon thought for a moment and then let out a deep breath.

"Let's push for an annulment with no strings first. If we don't get anywhere with that, then we offer her a job in exchange for annulment. If that fails, I'll agree to a divorce and some form of alimony. But we work in that order. Most important is that we get this done so we can all move on with our lives. And, Andrew, you make sure that I get joint custody of Antonio. Summers and vacations at the very least."

"Okay. Sounds like we have a plan. Let's go see if they are ready to resume negotiations. And, Brandon, let me do all the talking this time," said Andrew.

"I suppose I should. I pay you enough," said Brandon. He even offered a slight smile.

We didn't have a resolution yet, but there was a strategy. It was a strategy with outcomes that we could live with. We just had to see how Gina responded.

Chapter 15

Barbara indicated that she and Gina were ready to resume. When we were all gathered back in the conference room, Andrew asked Barbara to proceed. He wanted to see where they were before offering anything.

"As you are aware, we have mutually confirmed that there is no record of annulment filed with Italian officials. There remains, however, an official marriage certificate proving that that Ms. Arlotti and Mr. Mitchell were married ten years ago and remain legally married today. Are we to assume that Mr. Mitchell wants to end the marriage?"

"My office in Rome did a thorough investigation and we do not dispute your statement. My client and I accept it as fact," said Andrew. He leaned forward in his chair and placed his arms on the table.

"As for your question, you already know the answer. Yes, Mr. Mitchell intends to have the marriage annulled. That was the agreement between Ms. Arlotti and Mr. Mitchell ten years ago. My client believed that the appropriate action was taken at that time. We are merely seeking to correct the fact that no record of annulment can be located," said Andrew.

"So, Mr. Mitchell's position remains the same. As does Ms. Arlotti's. By virtue of Ms. Arlotti and Mr. Mitchell being legally married for ten years, and, may we remind you, a marriage that produced a son. A point of which no one is disputing," said Barbara.

"No. We are not disputing that. We do, nonetheless, need to wait for final confirmation from the paternity test," said Andrew.

"Understood," replied Barbara. "Nonetheless, my client and Mr. Mitchell have been legally married for ten years. We are confident that the courts would agree that this entitles my client to alimony."

"Under normal circumstances I would agree with you. In that case, I would advise my client to come to an alimony settlement. However, we are not dealing with normal circumstances. Neither Ms. Arlotti nor Mr. Mitchell intended to get married. They were both highly intoxicated at the time of the marriage. Frankly, I am amazed that a Justice of the Peace even performed a ceremony," said Andrew.

"But one did, and they are married," replied Barbara.

"True, but that does not change the indisputable fact that there was no real intent to get married. As soon as Ms. Arlotti and Mr. Mitchell sobered up the next day, they signed annulment papers. We cannot speak to why there is no longer a record of the annulment, but no one is denying that annulment papers were signed by both our clients," Andrew stated.

"Mr. Bennett, you know full well that all the courts will be concerned with is the presence of a marriage certificate and the absence of an annulment decree," said Barbara.

"Not so fast, Ms. Shay. There is, as I am sure you are aware, precedence in the Italian courts for the granting of an annulment when no real intent to get married is the issue. Even if a marriage is legally carried out, if it was done as a joke, or on a dare, or in other ways in which both parties did not intend to have an actual marriage. I think that any reasonable person can agree that this marriage, or lack thereof, meets that test."

The room fell silent. Barbara already knew everything that Andrew had stated. She had grasped at straws. A rather big mistake. Gina was visibly upset.

"There should be some recognition on the part of your client that Ms. Arlotti has been raising their son as a single parent for the past ten years. Some recognition on the part of your client that she deserves compensation."

Barbara Shay and Gina Arlotti were beat. They knew it. Barbara was doing her best to get something for her client.

"We can certainly go to court and make our cases there. That will not change the child support offer, but if your client strongly feels she deserves, and can win, alimony . . ." Andrew ended his statement with that.

Barbara whispered to Gina. Gina was defiant in her whispers back to Barbara. I had to assume that they had already gone over all of this during our break earlier. Perhaps Barbara had been unable to get Gina to agree too much of anything. Barbara held up her hand to Gina and then turned back to face us.

"What visitation or custody rights will your client seek?" Barbara asked.

"I don't believe that we have settled on the issue of annulment," replied Andrew.

Barbara may have been a partner at her law firm, but she seemed pretty bush league to me.

"We feel that is in the best interest of both our clients to come to an amicable agreement regarding the relationships involved. If Mr. Mitchell desires to receive generous visitation rights or some form of joint custody, then Ms. Arlotti is open to agreeing to an annulment," said Barbara.

Nice try to save your ass, I thought.

Andrew smiled and leaned forward. He placed his hands on the large mahogany table.

"Counselor," Andrew began, "do you really think that this particular strategy is in the best interest of your client? Once paternity is confirmed, my client will have rights as the boy's father. There would be no reason for the courts to deny him those rights."

"He has been an absentee father for all the boy's life up until this point," Barbara threw out as a hail Mary pass.

I had to bite my lip. I know that Brandon had done the same. I held his hand and gave it a squeeze.

"Until yesterday, my client was unaware that he had a son. Unaware because your client failed to inform him of that fact. My client has provided a more than generous child support package and will continue to provide for Antonio through college. He expressed his desire to be an active and positive participant in Antonio's life. To be a real dad to him. The question is not if my client will receive some measure of joint custody, but how much?"

"What is your client requesting?" asked Barbara.

"Summers and other school vacations. The ability to visit on weekends at other times as negotiated. We will also file the necessary paperwork to establish Antonio's joint citizenship in Italy and the United States," said Andrew.

"Fine. But we want the first child support payment immediately upon finalizing our agreement," said Barbara.

Gina stood and stormed out of the room.

"Is that going to be a problem?" Andrew asked Barbara.

"No. My client fully understands where we are at. She is, simply, unhappy with the outcome."

We stayed for a little longer to work out the details of Brandon and me meeting Antonio before he and Gina left New York. We also scheduled a trip to Italy. Brandon wanted to personally file the annulment paperwork and receive the decree. He suspected all along that Gina never filed the initial paperwork in case she ever desired to go after some of Brandon's fortune.

Brandon and I left Bennett, Sanders, & Ross hands-in-hand. We had smiles on our faces. We had received the best possible outcome and we were excited about meeting Antonio.

Back in our suite Brandon picked up the remote and turned on the gas fireplace. The room filled with the glow and warmth of the flames. I put on my robe and sat on the couch next to Brandon. He put his arm around my shoulders and pulled me close.

"How do you think Antonio will react to meeting us?" he asked.

"I don't know. I was never a ten-year-old boy. But I suspect he will feel a mix of emotions. Nervous, curious, excited. Don't get too worked up about the first meeting. He is meeting his father for the first time in his life. You are strangers. It will take time to get to know each other."

Brandon nodded.

"I just hope that I don't screw him up. I don't know the first thing about being a father."

"Yes, you do," I said. "You have a great example in your dad. Besides, you may be Mr. Big shot CEO, but you are a kind and caring man. If you truly love him, he will know it. That is the most important thing. The rest you will figure out as you go along."

"Do you think he likes baseball?" asked Brandon.

"I honestly don't know how big baseball is in Italy. I bet he likes James Bond and the Three Stooges though. That seems like a universal guy thing."

"He may be a little young for James Bond, but I bet he's seen the Stooges. I think I'll take him to a Yankees game. Smell of the grass, hot dogs, peanuts and Cracker Jacks."

"Can you smell all of those things from a luxury box?" I teased.

"Very funny . . . If you open the windows and there is a good breeze blowing in your direction you still get the smells," Brandon said with a smile. "The point is to experience a live Major League Baseball game."

"You are so cute," I said. "You want to bond with your son over a sport that you love. See? You will be a great dad."

We cuddled on the couch as we gazed into the flames as they danced in the fireplace. We talked more about Antonio and how we would build our life around having him in our family. We talked about having children together. We planned for the future. It felt good to be able to do that again.

As happy as I was in that moment, as excited as I was about meeting Antonio, I dreaded seeing Gina again. I didn't trust her. My woman's intuition was on overdrive. We would need to be guarded against her. While irrational, Gina felt that she was a woman scorned. Hell hath no fury . . .

Chapter 16

"How do I look?" asked Brandon.

I let out a loud laugh. Brandon had never, not once in four years, asked me how he looked. Brandon always knew exactly how to dress for any occasion. That ended the day he was going to meet his son for the first time.

The paternity test came back as we all expected it would. Brandon was, indeed, Antonio's father. We were relieved, actually. Now that the results were certain, we had become excited about Brandon being a dad.

"Brandon, you are going to meet your ten-year-old son. Short of you showing up in smelly gym clothes, I don't think he cares what you have on."

"Not helpful."

Wow. He was nervous. I couldn't believe it. My successful CEO was nervous. Would wonders never cease?

"I think khakis and a dress shirt is fine. You look great." I kissed Brandon on the cheek.

"Now, more importantly, what about me?" I asked. I twirled around.

"beautiful as ever."

"I wasn't exactly going for beautiful. He is a ten-year-old boy and my future stepson."

"You can't help it, Ash. You are always beautiful."

"You are sweet. But, seriously, how is this outfit?"

I was wearing a below the knee black skirt and a light blue blouse. It was one of my work outfits. It was both feminine and professional.

"You look super," said Brandon.

"Thanks."

"And beautiful." Brandon smiled.

We made our way to the hotel where Gina and Antonio were staying. Brandon was poking through the bag full of gifts that he had for Antonio. At last count, there was a Yankees baseball cap, an authentic Derek Jeter game jersey, a baseball glove, and a cell phone. I debated Brandon over a cell phone for a ten-year-old, but he said he wanted to be in easy contact with Antonio at all times.

Our car pulled up to the hotel, and we got out. We waited for Andrew to arrive and then made our way through the lobby and up to the private suite that Brandon had rented just for the occasion. Gina insisted on coming to the hotel. Brandon wanted to make it as neutral a setting as possible.

As we approached the door to the suite, I got a chill.

"She's already in there," I announced to Brandon.

"How do you know?"

"It's like I can sense an evil presence."

"I know she can be an ice queen, but evil might be a bit much."

I made no comment. We opened the door and entered.

Gina was seated on the sofa with Barbara Shay. Antonio was sitting on the floor watching Sponge Bob Square Pants on Nickelodeon. Gina spoke to him in Italian and he shut off the television. He stood and walked over near his mother.

In person, he looked even more like Brandon than in the photograph. Same jet-black hair. Same sparkling blue eyes. Same face. Same lips. He was a ten-year-old version of Brandon.

Antonio stood by Gina and nervously ran his finger up and down his leg. He cautiously looked over at us while simultaneously trying to avert his eyes. Curiosity mixed with fear. Barbara spoke softly to Antonio.

"Ciao, papà," Antonio said to Brandon.

"Ciao, il suo," replied Brandon.

I knew that exhausted Brandon's Italian. But he had practiced "Hello, son." Fortunately, Antonio spoke fluent English. Along with French, German, and, naturally, Italian.

I noticed that Brandon wiped a tear from the corner of his eye. I was near tears myself.

"Do you know Derek Jeter?" Antonio asked Brandon.

Everyone laughed. Well, almost everyone. Gina appeared to give a slight chuckle. She was probably afraid to let out a full smile or laugh for fear that it would crack her icy exterior.

"No. But look what I have for you," said Brandon as he pulled out the Yankees game jersey with Jeter and the number 2 on the back.

Antonio's eyes widened and a smile broke out across his face. He and Brandon met halfway and Brandon put the jersey on over Antonio's shirt.

"Here," Brandon said as he grabbed the Yankees cap and placed it on Antonio's head. "Complete the outfit."

We spent the rest of that morning getting acquainted with Antonio. There were obvious nerves, but everyone relaxed as we spent more time together. Antonio was smart, funny, and easy going. He was like Brandon in so many ways. My heart was bursting with joy. Just like that, we had a family.

Our meeting proceeded so well that Brandon and I took Antonio to lunch and followed up with a carriage ride through

Central Park. Antonio would need to return to Italy to finish his school year, but Brandon promised they would take in several Yankees games when Antonio came to stay with us for the summer. We had already decided that we would split our summer between New York and Santa Barbara.

When we returned to the hotel, Gina was less than thrilled that Antonio and Brandon hit it off so well. I think she secretly wanted Antonio to hate Brandon. I wouldn't have put it past her to have tried to poison Antonio's mind. If she had, it hadn't worked. Genuine affection and a bond were already forming between father and son.

We finalized the schedule for filing the annulment paperwork in Italy for the following week. Brandon invited Antonio to fly over to Italy with us. Gina at first denied the request, but Antonio begged her to let him fly on a private jet. She relented.

We said goodbye for the afternoon. Both Brandon and I got big hugs from Antonio. As we left the hotel, we were both in tears. Tears of joy at having Antonio in our life, and tears of sorrow that we wouldn't be with him every day.

Chapter 17

"Honey, are you ready?" Brandon called out to me.

"Coming," I said. I padded down the hall as I pulled my suitcases behind me.

"Sure you packed enough?" Brandon asked sarcastically.

"It's only a week in Italy, so I packed light."

Brandon rolled his eyes.

"How many trips have we taken together?" I asked.

"Okay. I should be used to how you pack by now." Brandon helped with my luggage and headed toward the door.

I followed Brandon out the door and down to the waiting town car. When we picked up Antonio from the hotel, he was wearing his New York Yankees baseball cap.

"Like father, like son," I commented to Brandon with a smile.

As we headed to the airport, Antonio looked in amazement at all the tall buildings. But nothing compared to his wide-eyed amazement as we pulled into the private hanger.

"Wow. Cool," he said when he saw the Lear jet.

"Is it really just for us?" he asked.

"Yep," answered Brandon.

"Imponente!" shouted Antonio as he jumped out of the car and ran toward the jet.

"Did he just say impotent?" asked Brandon.

"My Italian is rusty, but I think he said 'awesome,'" I replied.

Brandon nodded his head. "That would make more sense."

We boarded the plane. Antonio looked around the cabin.

"What does a plane like this cost?" Antonio asked.

"Truly like father, like son," I said with a laugh.

"About six million dollars or 4.8 million euros," said Brandon.

Antonio nodded his head like he fully appreciated how much money that was. Of course, he was Brandon's son.

Brandon's pilot showed Antonio the cockpit and explained some of the pre-flight checks. Antonio absorbed it all like a sponge.

We settled into our seats for takeoff. Once we were in the air and leveled off, we were served lunch. Antonio had a cheeseburger.

"This is really good," Antonio said between bites.

"I'm glad you like it," said Brandon.

After we finished eating, he sat and looked at Brandon and me for a moment.

"Can I ask you something?" he asked me.

"Sure," I said.

"You are marrying my dad, right?"

"Yes."

"So that will make you his wife?"

"Yes."

"Will that make you my other mom?"

"Well, I wouldn't try to be your mom. But I will be your step mom. Partly your mom through marriage."

"Oh, okay. You are very pretty."

"Thank you, Antonio. And you are every bit as handsome as your dad," I said.

We talked about Antonio's school and what he liked to do for fun. He asked us many questions about what it would be like when he came to stay with us for the summer. He wanted to know if he was attending our wedding. Brandon asked him to be our ring bearer, and he was thrilled to have a role to play in our special day. After a few hours, Antonio stretched out on the couch and took a nap.

About half way through the flight, Brandon and I caught a nap ourselves. Almost nine hours after we left New York, we landed in Milan. We had a car waiting for us at the airport and took Antonio home.

"Looks like Gina has done okay for herself," I whispered in Brandon's ear as we pulled up to the house.

It was a nice home in an upscale neighborhood. A nanny came out of the front door to greet us. Gina stood at the open doorway and glared at us.

"Did the temperature just drop thirty degrees?" asked Brandon.

"See? She sends off bad vibes," I said.

Antonio hugged us goodbye. We told him that we would pick him up after lunch the next day. He hugged his Nanny and then went toward the open front door.

Gina simply patted Antonio on the head like he was a puppy. He brushed by her like that was the typical greeting he received from her.

"We will meet you at 10:00 A.M. to file the annulment papers," Brandon said to Gina.

"Bene," Gina replied.

"Fine?" Brandon asked me.

"Yes."

He nodded his head. We got back in the car and headed to our hotel. Milan was a city filled with culture, and I hoped that we would have some time to take in the sights during our visit.

Mostly, though, I would be relieved to have the annulment finalized. Then we could truly get on with our lives.

Chapter 18

Gina met us at ten o'clock and we filed the annulment paperwork without incident. Brandon waited to receive an annulment certificate. Gina asked Brandon if he had deposited the first child support payment. He told her that the deposit was made earlier that morning into her bank account. Gina pulled up the account on her iPhone to check.

"Buono," was all that Gina said.

"We will be by after lunch to pick Antonio up. We are going to the park and out for ice cream," Brandon confirmed with Gina.

Gina simply nodded her head and went on her way.

"Seems all she cares about is getting the money in her bank account," I said.

"Doesn't matter. The annulment is done and we have Antonio for summers and other vacations."

Brandon and I kissed. I was tense.

"Hey, relax," Brandon said to me. "Everything has worked out."

"Woman's intuition. I don't trust Gina. I get a really bad feeling when I am around her."

"Let's get some lunch and look forward to our afternoon with Antonio."

Brandon kissed me again. I smiled and held him close.

We had a nice lunch that went a long way toward making me feel better. After lunch, we went to pick Antonio up. We rang the bell and no one answered. Brandon knocked on the door.

Brandon took out his cell phone and dialed Gina's number. No answer. He called the phone that he had given Antonio. It just rang. No answer. No voice mail.

We peeked in the front window. The house was dark. I had a bad feeling in the pit of my stomach.

"Mr. Mitchell!" We turned toward the street. It was Antonio's nanny. Her eyes were puffy and red. Tears ran down her face.

"Se ne sono andati! Se ne sono andati!" she exclaimed.

"In English," said Brandon.

"They are gone!" she repeated in English.

"Gone?" asked Brandon.

"I went out to run errands. When I came back, they were gone."

"You mean, they are out somewhere?" I asked.

"No. They left. They packed some clothes and left. Ms. Gina left a note saying they no longer needed me. They were leaving Milan."

"When was this? How long ago?" asked Brandon.

"About an hour. I knew you and Ms. Sullivan were coming by so I waited at the café across the street. Mr. Mitchell, where could they go? Why?"

"I don't know."

That feeling that I had in the pit of my stomach turned into full blown panic. Gina Arlotti had left with Antonio. I had no doubt that she did not want us to find them.

Chapter 19

Brandon and I sat in the Milan police department with one of their detectives. Bennett, Sanders, & Ross sent one of the attorneys, Lorenzo Bertani, from their office in Rome to assist us. We provided all the legal paperwork that proved Brandon was Antonio's father and that we had both child support and custody agreements with Gina Arlotti. The police would start an investigation, but Brandon wanted things to move faster.

"So, what are our options?" Brandon asked Lorenzo Bertani.

"The police will do what they can, but it may take some time to locate Ms. Arlotti and your son. They are free to move about Italy and throughout the European Union. The police will get word out that Antonio is traveling with one parent without the authorization of the second parent. They will be stopped if they try to cross a border."

"But if they have already left Italy?" asked Brandon.

"Unless they try to cross another border . . . it may take longer to locate them," replied Lorenzo.

"I know the police are doing all they can, but we need more resources on this," said Brandon. "I want to hire a private investigator to start looking. Who do you recommend?"

"We use the Galletta Detective Agency in Rome whenever we need any investigative work done. They are excellent. They also have offices all over Europe. In fact, I believe they even have an office here in Milan," replied Lorenzo.

"Good. Please put me in touch with them."

"I will have someone from their office contact you shortly."

"Thank you."

"I am available to assist with any legal filings once we locate your son. I assure you that, at a minimum, the joint custody arrangement will be enforced," stated Lorenzo.

"Is there a chance we could gain primary custody?" I asked.

"If it turns out that Ms. Arlotti was trying to flee with Antonio? I believe there would be a strong case to be made. But this not a typical divorce and joint custody situation, so it is too soon to say exactly what would happen. Let's concentrate on locating Antonio first," said Lorenzo. "Let me call my office so we can get the ball rolling on hiring the investigators."

Within ten minutes Brandon received a call from Marco Galletti of the Galletti Detective Agency. He was the President of the agency, based in Rome. He gave Brandon the address of their Milan office and stated that his head detective in Milan, Matteo Silvi, was expecting us and would handle the investigation. Marco Galletti assured Brandon that Matteo Silvi was a top detective and specialized in finding missing persons.

"Their Milan office is actually only a few blocks from here. Their head detective is waiting for us," Brandon told me.

There was nothing more for Lorenzo to do at the moment, so he left to return to Rome. Brandon and I walked the two blocks to the Galletti Detective Agency's Milan office. It was located on the third floor of a small office building. Brandon and I took the elevator to the third floor.

Brandon tapped his foot nervously and I reached over to hold his hand.

"Everything will be okay. We will find Antonio. Whatever it takes," I said.

"There are only two people who have had an instant hold me on. You . . . and Antonio," Brandon said.

"Brandon, he's your son. It doesn't matter that you only found out about him last week and met him for the first time a few days ago. We will find him."

The elevator stopped on the third floor and we got out. We crossed the hall and entered the lobby of Galletti Detective Agency.

"Buon pomeriggio, signore. Come posso aiutarla?" greeted the receptionist.

"Brandon Mitchell to see Marco Silvi," replied Brandon.

"Yes, sir. Just a moment," the receptionist replied in perfect English.

I was always a bit embarrassed when we traveled internationally. Most people where we visited spoke English. I barely passed Spanish in high school. Brandon spoke French fairly well, but not Italian.

"Mr. Mitchell, I am Marco Salvini. It is a pleasure to meet you, although I am sorry for the circumstances," said Marco Salvini as he stepped out of his office.

Brandon shook his hand.

"This is my fiancée, Ashley Sullivan."

Marco greeted me as well.

"Please. Let's discuss your case in my office. May we offer you any refreshments?" asked Marco.

"No. Thank you," we replied.

Marco sat behind his desk and we sat in the two chairs opposite him.

"Your attorney has already sent us pictures of your son Antonio and his mother. Of course, most people in Italy know of Gina Arlotti. Until a few years ago, she was still a top model," said Marco.

"Will that make it easier to find them?" asked Brandon.

"Perhaps. It depends where she has gone and who she may be with. If she is already staying with a friend or family somewhere, she could remain hidden for quite some time," replied Marco.

"So how do you plan on finding them?" asked Brandon.

"We will question neighbors, family, friends, and known associates. I also think we should go to the media. Perhaps someone saw them recently. It may help us narrow the area in which we search. But the police will do all of that as well. We, of course, will work with them as much as possible. Nonetheless, it is always helpful to talk to people on our own. People sometimes remember different things at different times."

"Fine. What else?" asked Brandon.

"Do you have a cell phone number for Ms. Arlotti?" asked Marco.

"Yes. One for Antonio as well. I just gave him the phone the other day," replied Brandon. "But I'm not sure what good calling them will do. Gina won't answer. I'm sure she will not let Antonio use his either. I've called him several times. His phone is off."

"Yes, but at some point Ms. Arlotti is likely to use her phone. Or your son will turn it on to play a game or watch a video on YouTube. You know how kids are. He may not defy her and try to contact you, but games, the Internet, and such are too tempting," replied Marco.

"I'm sorry to be short with you, but what is your point?" said Brandon.

"I understand your frustration, Mr. Mitchell. If a cell phone is on, it has a signal that can be traced. We follow the phone's GPS signal in reverse."

"So we could get an exact location?" I asked.

"Yes. If the phone is on and we are able to lock in on the signal. It takes a little doing, but I'm sure we can work with the police and wireless carrier."

"Won't the police already be doing that?" asked Brandon.

"Probably. But two pairs of eyes and ears are better than one. Our agency can monitor 24/7. We also have offices all over Europe and can respond very quickly to a location. Working in partnership with the police, we can cover all the bases," said Marco.

"Then let's get to work," said Brandon. He gave Marco both Gina and Antonio's cell phone numbers. He also provided all the details on Antonio's wireless account.

Brandon and I left and headed back to our hotel. We felt helpless, but there was nothing more we could do at that moment. I held his hand tightly. I don't think that I had ever seen Brandon shaken so deeply before. I was worried. But after speaking with Marco, at least I now had hope.

Chapter 20

Several hours had passed when Brandon's cell phone rang. Marco Silvi was on the phone.

"We have a location. About thirty minutes outside of Milan. We are en route and have alerted the local police. I will pick you up at your hotel in ten minutes," said Marco.

"Thank you. We will be out front when you get here," said Brandon. He hung up.

"That was Marco. They have a location. He will be here in ten minutes to pick us up."

Brandon and I made our way down to the hotel lobby and out the front door. Marco was right on time. We got in his car and were on our way.

"Do we know for certain that Gina and Antonio are still at the location?" Brandon asked as soon as we were in the car.

"Yes. Gina made a call on her cell phone. Antonio's phone also gave a signal. We picked up the signals right away. The local police have already arrived," replied Marco.

"Where are they?" I asked.

"One of Ms. Arlotti's cousins. It's not clear if Ms. Arlotti planned on traveling further," Marco said.

Thirty minutes later, we arrived at Gina's cousin's house. A police car was parked out front. We approached the front door. A police officer answered. Marco showed identification and they had a short conversation in Italian. The officer then stepped aside and allowed us to enter the house.

Gina, Antonio, and a woman I assumed was Gina's cousin, sat in the living room. A second police officer stood in one corner of the living room. Antonio looked confused. However, he seemed okay. He was speaking with one of the police officers and showing him something on his cell phone. Gina looked pissed. Gina's cousin looked like a deer in headlights.

Antonio looked up as we entered the tiny living room.

"Papa and Miss Ashley!" he exclaimed. "Did you see the police car? Pretty cool, huh?"

"Yes, son," said Brandon. "Let me speak with your mother for a few minutes."

"Why don't we go into the kitchen," suggested Marco.

Gina, Brandon, Marco, and I went into the small kitchen. The police officer who greeted us at the door followed us in. We closed the kitchen door.

"Just what the hell were you thinking?!" said Brandon to Gina. "Where, exactly, were you planning to go with Antonio?"

"I just needed a few days to think. Everything has changed so fast," said Gina.

"Then why did you tell your Nanny that you no longer needed her services and were leaving Milan?" asked Brandon.

"That little snitch," said Gina.

"Did you think no one would question her?" asked Brandon.

"It's why I didn't tell her where we were going."

Gina didn't seem to be under arrest, so no one had informed her of her legal right to remain silent. At least I assumed they had that in Italy. At any rate, Gina wasn't doing herself any favors.

"Ms. Arlotti, you were traveling with your minor son without the permission of his second parent," said Marco.

"So, what, am I under arrest?"

"Not at present. But much of what happens depends on how Mr. Mitchell chooses to proceed. Then it is up to the legal system to decide," answered Marco.

"You have got to be shittin' me. I can't even travel with my own son?" asked Gina.

"You share custody with Mr. Mitchell. So, no, you can't just travel without his knowledge. It could be considered kidnapping," replied Marco.

"What?!" said Gina.

She turned to the police officer.

"È vero?" she asked him.

Marco told us that she asked the police officer if that was true. The police officer responded that he was not a lawyer, but she could be brought in for questioning and possibly charged with taking her son without knowledge of the other parent. Marco translated that as well for us.

"Gina, despite you being a royal pain in my ass, I have no desire to see you charged. As much as it may amuse me to see you spend some time in jail, I'm not sure that is in Antonio's best interest. So, we are going to get to the bottom of this and decide what to do next," said Brandon.

Marco explained to the police officer that no charges were going to be filed at present. The police officer took Brandon's information for his report and then left.

"Do you need me for anything else?" asked Marco.

"No. Thank you for your assistance and so quickly locating my son," replied Brandon.

"It has been my pleasure. Would you like me to wait to drive you back to Milan?"

"No. Thank you. I will arrange for a car service to take us back."

"Very well. Enjoy the rest of your time in Italy. Arrivederci. Goodbye," said Marco.

"Arrivederci," Brandon and I said.

Marco left. Brandon and I sat at the kitchen table with Gina.

"Okay, tell us what is going on," said Brandon.

Gina looked down at her hands.

"You wouldn't understand," she said.

"Try me," said Brandon.

"You couldn't possibly understand my situation," she said.

"Look, Gina, I'm in no mood for games. Just tell me what is going on."

"I don't need you to judge me. I did the only thing I could think of to take care of Antonio. I have no skills beyond being a model. What was I supposed to do when my career to an abrupt end?"

"Okay, so you thought about me and that I would be of some value in providing child support for Antonio. I don't fault you for that. In fact, I wish I had known about Antonio all along. I could have been in his life before now. I could have been providing the very best for him all along."

"I thought about contacting you when I found out that I was pregnant. But my career was going so well. After I had Antonio, I quickly got back in modeling shape and things continued to go very well. I hired a nanny. I liked my life. I saw no need to complicate it with paternity issues."

"But you gave little thought to my right to know that I had a son?"

"You said that you wouldn't judge me."

"I'm just having a hard time coming to terms with the fact that you withheld Antonio from me for ten years. Nonetheless, continuing to dwell on that will not change anything. We need to find a way to move forward from where we are now," said Brandon.

Gina continued to stare at her hands. She was unable to make eye contact. My opinion about her changed somewhat. Gina seemed ashamed.

"I'm broke. Apart from the child support you just paid, I have no money," she said.

"So you ran? I don't understand," said Brandon.

"My modeling career is over. It has been over for some months now. I have spent what little savings I had. I have never been good with money. Spending what I made or more."

"Okay, I follow you so far," said Brandon.

"I saw the news of your engagement on the *Jacqueline* website. I started thinking that I could use the situation to my advantage. I had little doubt that I could get child support for Antonio, but I . . . I thought . . ."

Gina fumbled with her hands. A tear began to form in the corner of her eye. She didn't seem talented enough to fake it, so I believed the tear was genuine.

Gina continued, "I thought that if I could receive alimony . . . it would be enough for me to live on rather comfortably."

"But, for that, we would still need to be married. I know that we filed the annulment. I never understood how there could be no record of it. Believe me. My attorneys did a thorough search." Brandon stared hard at Gina's lowered head.

Gina, for the first time, looked up. Tears streamed down her cheeks. I saw a woman who had been desperate, but I was still having trouble with the fact that she played with our emotions and tried to disrupt my marrying Brandon.

"My cousin, Isabella, works in the records department. I asked her to delete the annulment record from the live computer system. There are backups of the record and an archived paper copy, but I figured no one would think to look any further than the official main database system."

"You what?! Gina! How could you even think to do that to me? To Ashley? Not to mention that you broke at least a few laws in the process. Maybe some jail time would do you some good!"

"Brandon, no, please! I beg you. Please try to see it from my point of view."

"Your point of view? Your point of view? What, the one where you devised a scam to erase a public record and then extort false alimony payments out of me? That point of view?"

Brandon stood up. He paced across the kitchen. He ran his hand along his face. He let out a deep sigh.

"I don't even know what to do with this information," said Brandon. "I don't know what to do about you."

I was in shock. I couldn't believe that Gina orchestrated a scam like that. I get that she felt desperate, but I couldn't even think to do what she had done. Not that I am perfect, but, jjeez.

"How can a record simply be deleted so easily like that?" Brandon asked.

"It's not that easy. You can't just hit delete. But if you understand the software, there are ways. Isabella works in the IT department. She understands all that stuff," Gina said.

"I don't understand you, Gina," said Brandon. "You really thought there was nothing else you could have done with your life after modeling? Absolutely nothing? You had to resort to this?"

Gina was crying. Brandon was furious. I was shocked. I had no idea what we were going to do with this new information.

"So what do we do?" I asked.

"I'm not sure," Brandon replied.

Chapter 21

Antonio left with us to go back to Milan. Gina offered no objection when Brandon demanded that Antonio stay with us for a few days. Not that she had much of a choice. We held all the cards.

Antonio played a video game in the second bedroom of our suite at the hotel. Brandon and I sat in the living room as we contemplated next steps.

"Brandon, I know that Gina broke the law. I know that she attempted to receive alimony falsely . . ."

"Which is fraud, in and of itself."

"Yes. I understand that. Look, I am every bit as upset about all of this as you are. The woman played with our emotions. She attempted to hold our wedding hostage," I said.

"Why do I feel a but coming?" said Brandon.

"But we need to think about what is going to work best going forward. How do we protect Antonio? Gina is unpredictable. So how do we protect Antonio and enforce the joint custody?"

"We could go to the police with what we now know," replied Brandon.

"We could."

"But? . . ."

"She was desperate. What she did was wrong. Nonetheless, I don't want to get caught up in filing charges and court cases here in Italy. What would that do to Antonio? Think about that. What would his mother being on trial and possibly going to jail do to him?"

"As usual, you're right," said Brandon. "He already has enough changes in his life."

"Yes, he does. But they are good changes. He is getting to know his father. He has financial security and a bright future ahead of him," I said.

"We just need to find a way to protect that. I don't trust Gina. Joint custody of summers and vacations won't work any longer. It also will not work having Antonio living in Italy with Gina. We need to find a way to bring him to the States," said Brandon.

"Do we try to get full custody with visitation rights for Gina?" I asked.

"How do you feel about that? It would make us instant full-time parents."

"Brandon, I want what is best for Antonio. It would be an adjustment for all of us, but I think it would be wonderful."

"Ashley Sullivan, you are the most amazing woman." Brandon kissed me and held me close. Everything felt better when I was in his arms.

"What about Gina?" I asked.

"She is not the most amazing woman," replied Brandon.

"You know that is not what I meant."

"The opportunity presented itself."

"So nice that you still have your twisted sense of humor," I said, "but we do need to figure out how we are going to deal with Gina."

"Given everything that has happened, I have no doubt we can win full custody. You're right that prosecuting her could be very negative for Antonio. If not for him... . But, yes, how it affects Antonio is most definitely a factor."

Brandon crossed the living room and gazed out the window over Milan. Many people do their best thinking in the shower. Brandon seemed to do his best thinking as he looked out a window.

"Frankly, I would prefer to let her fend for herself in Italy," said Brandon. "However, Antonio should be able to see his mother on a regular basis. Both Gina and I need to be present and active in his life. It will be least disruptive to him."

"See, you are thinking like a true parent," I said with a smile. "So, we find a way to make it possible for Gina to move to the United States? Live close to us?"

"She doesn't seem to have any prospects here in Italy. If we provide one for her in Santa Barbara . . ."

"A job at *Jacqueline*?"

"Yes. But I cannot take credit for the idea. A very wise woman had suggested it as an option the other day."

"Really?" I said with a grin. "And who might that have been?"

Brandon put his arms around my waist and drew me close to him. He gazed into my eyes. His gorgeous blue eyes sparkled like the ocean.

"An incredibly beautiful and vivacious woman who also happens to be incredible in bed."

"Is that so?"

"Yes. And I hope that she will remind me of just how incredible later tonight."

"I think that can be arranged."

We kissed. Brandon's lips were soft and warm. His arms held me strong.

"Ooh, gross."

We turned and Antonio stood near the couch.

"I guess we will need to get used to having a ten-year-old boy in the house," I said with a smile.

"Yes. And girls are still icky at that age," said Brandon.

"Can I have a snack?" Antonio asked.

"Of course," I said.

"Why don't we all go out for some gelato?" said Brandon.

"Yeah, gelato," said Antonio with a large smile. He smiled just like Brandon.

"Then there is something that we would like to discuss with you," said Brandon.

Chapter 22

"So I would live in California? And Mamma would too?" asked Antonio.

"Yes. That would be the idea," replied Brandon.

"But I would live with you and Miss Ashley? When would I see Mamma?"

"Well, you could see her every day. We will make sure she lives very close to us," said Brandon.

"I think that I would like living with you, but . . ."

"Why would you live with us and not your mother?" I said.

"Yes," replied Antonio.

"Well, there are complicated legal reasons. It makes it easier for you moving to the United States to live with your dad and me," I said.

I had no other way to explain it to Antonio. Technically what I said was true. He was too young to understand fully what was going on. Plus, there was no need to drag his mother's name through the mud.

"We promise that you will see your mother every day. Besides, we will be able to enroll you at Santa Barbara Academy. It is a wonderful school."

"You will make many wonderful friends there," I added.

"And we can go to the beach? And boating?" asked Antonio.

"Yes. Lots," said Brandon.

"Will you take me to school in your sports car?"

"The Aston Martin? Sure. Probably not every day. But whenever I can," said Brandon.

"Cool," said Antonio.

"And Mamma would work at your magazine?"

"Yes. We have yet to define her exact role, but her experience as a model can be utilized," said Brandon.

"Huh?" said Antonio.

"Brandon, sweetie, Antonio is a very smart boy. But you have to remember that he is ten," I said.

"Right. Yes, your mom would work at *Jacqueline*. An important job based on her years as a model."

"So what do you think?" Brandon asked Antonio.

"As long as Mamma is coming, I guess it is okay."

"Excellent. Now, let's finish these gelatos and get back to the hotel. We need to finalize plans with your mother," said Brandon.

Chapter 23

Gina took what we told her much better than expected. She realized that she had created a significant legal problem for herself and had been offered a very nice "get out of jail free" card. I had even sensed some relief from her. I know that she would have preferred to have retained more custody of Antonio, but getting to see him every day was much better than the likely alternative. Had we gone through the court system, Gina would have fared far worse.

Bennett, Sanders, & Ross handled all the legal paperwork with relative ease. The Davenport Board of Directors were less than thrilled in moving up the schedule to relocate Brandon's office to Santa Barbara, but we felt it least disruptive for Antonio. As a bonus, it would make wedding planning easier.

Brandon and I sat on the patio of our suite at Lusso. Antonio was at the pool with Chelsea. Chelsea had arrived the night before to assist with some of the wedding plans. I particularly wanted her with me when I bought my wedding dress. I was also hoping to convince her to come work as legal counsel at the Mitchell Family Foundation that Brandon and I had decided to start after we were married.

"Okay, so what's on the schedule for today?" Brandon asked me.

"Lunch and wedding dress shopping with Chelsea. You have Antonio for the afternoon to do guy stuff."

"I think we'll go out for pizza and then hit the batting cages," said Brandon.

"Sounds like fun," I said. "We have an appointment with the wedding planner here at Lusso tomorrow morning. Did Steve find us some houses to look at for the afternoon?"

Steve was our real estate agent. As much as we loved staying at the Lusso, we were anxious to purchase a house.

"Yes. He has two great houses. Both waterfront estates with private beach access."

"How close to Santa Barbara Academy?"

"Both are within a few miles."

"So they would be close to Gina's townhouse as well?"

We just got Gina settled into a nice townhouse. Brandon covered her first month's rent until she started collecting her paycheck from her new job at *Jacqueline*. Brandon decided that her job was advising the magazine on European fashion. She was actually making positive contributions.

"Yes. Her townhouse is actually in between the school and both the houses. Would work out well either way."

The door to the suite opened and we could hear Chelsea and Antonio's laughter. It was an easy sell convincing Antonio to go to the pool with Chelsea. Ten-year-old girls may still have been icky, but Antonio's reaction to Chelsea was the same as every other straight male.

"How was the pool?" I asked.

"Great!" said Antonio as he stared adoringly at Chelsea.

"Why don't you get changed," said Brandon. "I thought we would grab a pizza and then hit some balls at the batting cages."

"Awesome. Can Miss Chelsea come?"

"Sorry," said Chelsea. "I'm helping Ashley choose her wedding dress."

"Oh. Okay." Antonio hung his head in complete disappointment.

"Hey," said Brandon, "I know I'm not as good looking as Chelsea, but don't seem so disappointed to spend the afternoon with your dad."

"Sorry, Dad. You're fun too."

"I'll see you tonight for dinner," Chelsea said to Antonio.

A smile returned to Antonio's face.

"Awesome. See you later, then."

"See you later, cutie," said Chelsea.

Antonio padded into his bedroom to change.

"He is so cute," said Chelsea.

"Well, you have definitely made an impression on him," I said.

"He just has exquisite taste," said Chelsea with a grin. "Let me run to my room and shower and get dressed."

"Just swing back around when you're ready. Maria is so excited to see us," I said.

Maria was a former Italian model and owned Maria's Dress Boutique in downtown Santa Barbara. I had worked at Maria's while I was in college. Maria had been like a second mother to me. It was the only place that I considered for my wedding dress.

"Give me twenty minutes," said Chelsea.

Chelsea left and Brandon turned to me with a naughty look in his eyes.

"So, we have twenty minutes . . ." said Brandon.

"Not so fast," I said as I held up my hand. "As tempting as that may be, and it is, we do not have twenty minutes. We probably have about two minutes before Antonio is ready for pizza and the batting cages."

"Well, that's a little fast, but . . ."

"Get out of here," I said with a laugh.

"Okay, but you owe me a rain check for later."

Antonio walked back into the living room. He was wearing jeans, his Derek Jeter baseball jersey, and a Yankees baseball cap.

"What's a rain check?" he asked.

"A promise to get something later," said Brandon.

"Get what later?"

"Um . . . dessert," said Brandon.

"I want a rain check for dessert," said Antonio.

"Don't worry, son. You can have cake, ice cream, or whatever you want for dessert after dinner this evening," said Brandon.

"Even that double fudge cake they have in the restaurant downstairs?" asked Antonio.

"Absolutely," replied Brandon. "Now, who's hungry for pizza?"

"I am! Can we get pepperoni?" asked Antonio.

"Pepperoni it is," said Brandon.

Chapter 24

Chelsea and I sat at one of our favorite downtown Santa Barbara restaurants.

"This brings back a lot of memories," said Chelsea.

"It sure does. I knew that I missed living here, but I didn't realize just how much," I said.

"Ash, everything has changed so fast. You're doing such an amazing job of dealing with it all."

"Thanks. At first it was a nightmare. Gina showing up the way she did. But look at what has come out of it. Antonio is such an amazing kid. I just love him. And Brandon is really embracing being a dad."

"I don't know if I would have handled it as well as you have."

"I'm sure Gina would not have come out as unscathed if you were let loose on her," I said.

Chelsea was an absolute doll. Unless you crossed her. Then she could be a pit bull. Especially if you hurt someone she cared about.

"Why, whatever do you mean?" Chelsea asked with a coy smile.

"Do you recall a former college boyfriend of mine who would cross to the other side of campus just to avoid you?"

"Which one?"

"My point exactly," I said. "Of course there were only two. But both feared you."

I hadn't had the best of luck in the boyfriend department in college. But Chelsea was always there to pick me up. She also struck a little fear into the hearts of those who had crushed mine.

"How do you think it's all going to work out with Gina? I mean, she did try to take Antonio away," said Chelsea.

"It's only been a few weeks. But so far, so good," I said. "There really isn't any wiggle room for her to mess up. Brandon has control over her passport and work visa. So she can't get out of the country without Brandon knowing in advance. Gina also knows if she were to try to take Antonio again, she would spend time in jail and it would be a long time before she ever saw him again."

"Pretty big incentive to stay on the straight and narrow," said Chelsea.

"Yes. Now, let's talk about something else."

"Like that you have a wedding to plan," said Chelsea.

"And you need to help," I said. "But, before that, there is something else I wanted to talk to you about."

"Sounds serious."

"It is. But good serious," I said.

"Okay. What is it?"

"Brandon and I have decided to start a family foundation after we're married. The Mitchell Family Foundation. It will handle all of our charity work, including our funding for the arts."

"What about the Davenport Foundation?" asked Chelsea.

"That will still exist. But Brandon and I wanted something that was uniquely ours. We will, however, shift much of the funding for the Davenport School of the Arts, and Santa Barbara University more broadly, to the new foundation."

"That makes sense, given your connection to both the School of the Arts and the university."

"I know. Can you believe that we've been out of college four years now?" I asked.

"But we still look as good as we did then," said Chelsea.

"Better."

"I'll drink to that," said Chelsea.

"Well, there is something else I would like you to drink to," I said.

"What's that?"

"You joining the foundation as legal counsel," I said.

"What? Are you serious?"

"Yes. Chels, think about it. There is no one I would trust more than you. You've already passed the California Bar Exam. It would also allow you time to teach some courses at Santa Barbara University."

"I don't know what to say," she said.

"Being a non-profit, the foundation won't be able to pay as much as a law firm, but it will pay you top dollar for the non-profit sector. It would still be a great salary, plus a terrific benefits package. Chels, we could work together every day."

"So you'd be at the foundation every day?"

"Yes. Oh, I forgot to mention that part. I will be leaving *Jacqueline* to run the foundation."

"But you love your job at *Jacqueline*. It was your dream job."

"True. But I really want to give back. I'll still have a say in things at *Jacqueline*, but the foundation has become a passion of mine."

"I don't know about us working together. Technically, working for you," said Chelsea.

"Technically, yes. But, Chels, come on, do you really see that being an issue? You would be legal counsel. You would be there to provide your legal expertise to everything the foundation does. I'd rely on you for that. I don't really see it as you working for me, per se."

"I'll have to think about it."

"Take all the time you need," I said. "Just please say yes," I begged.

Chelsea smiled and shook her head.

"You know how hard it is for me to say 'no' to you," she said.

"That's what I am counting on," I said as I smiled back at her.

Chapter 25

"Ciao. E 'così bello vederti!" greeted Maria as Chelsea and I walked into her dress shop.

"Cio, Maria. It is wonderful to see you as well," I said. We all hugged.

"Let me look at you," said Maria. "Così bella. So beautiful."

"You are sweet," I said.

"I am excited to fit you for your wedding dress," said Maria. Then she looked at Chelsea.

"Can you believe it? Ashley marrying Brandon Mitchell. Magnifico!" exclaimed Maria.

"Hmm, if I recall correctly, you were not so excited when I was going on my first date with him," I said.

"I don't recall," said Maria with a coy smile.

"Oh, I do," I said.

"Me too," said Chelsea.

Maria gave a dismissive wave of her hand and smiled.

"Come. Take a look at the wedding gown collection," she said as she took me by the hand.

"Maria, they are all so beautiful. How will I ever choose?"

"You will know when you have found the perfect dress for you," she replied.

"This could take a while," I said.

"We have all afternoon," said Chelsea.

Maria began pulling dresses off the rack for me to look at. I selected one and tried it on. Then another. And another after that. They were all wonderful, but I hadn't felt like I found the perfect dress. I had a momentary twinge about my mom not being there but it was a fleeting one.

I knew my parents were pinching their pennies for the wedding after turning down our offer to fly them to Santa Barbara. My dad was making good money again, but they were also trying to build up a retirement account. But I knew it was a source of pride to him that they not accept our attempts to help out any more financially than I had before.

To be honest, it was probably for the best. My mother had dreamed about me walking down the aisle in a puffy, multi-layered dress reminiscent like her own wedding gown. I wanted to be a princess on my wedding day. But I also wanted to be modern and stylish as well. While I respected my mother's opinion, there might have been hurt feelings if I had not gone with a gown she selected.

"Here," said Chelsea.

"What about this one?" She held up a Maggie Sottero.

"That is a wonderful choice," said Maria. "It is the Pilar dress. A timeless and classic look. Very elegant."

"It is beautiful. I love the classic look. Let me try it on," I said.

I took the dress into the changing room. When I came back out, both Chelsea and Maria were speechless for a moment. I twirled to give them a look at the back as well.

"You are absolutely radiant," said Chelsea.

"Splendido. Gorgeous," said Maria.

The dress was a slim A-line wedding gown. It was fashioned with delicate lace and ethereal tulle. It had scalloped trim that adorned the V-neckline and a plunging back. It fit me perfectly.

"Ash, it is you. Classic, elegant, and beautiful," said Chelsea.

"I love it," I said. "This is the dress."

"Magnifico!" exclaimed Maria. "Let me check the measurements, but I don't think I will even need to touch it. Seems like a perfect fit."

Maria inspected the length and how the dress fit against me. She said she wouldn't dare touch it.

"As long as you don't gain any weight, or grow or shrink," Maria said, "it is a perfect fit. I wouldn't dare touch it."

"See how much I value your opinion," I said to Chelsea.

Chelsea simply nodded her head and smiled.

Chapter 26

"Let's get a move on," Brandon called to Antonio.

Antonio rushed into the living room of the suite.

"Are we taking the Aston Martin?" he asked hopefully.

"Not today, buddy," replied Brandon.

"Bummer," said Antonio.

"It's a two-seater. Where would Ashley sit?"

"Where would Ashley sit?" I asked.

"Well, Antonio is my co-pilot."

"Oh, I see how this works now," I said with a smile.

Brandon smiled and gave me a kiss on the cheek.

"We are going to take my new car," I said.

I had just purchased a Mercedes E-400 hybrid sedan. It was Diamond White Metallic with black leather interior.

"It has new car smell and a panorama sunroof," I said trying to cheer Antonio up.

"What's that?" asked Antonio.

"The panorama sunroof?"

He nodded his head.

"A glass sunroof in both the front and back seats," I said. "You can open the sunroof in back if you want."

Antonio grinned at me. Score. Taking my car met with Antonio's approval. I was excited to drive it. I had never owned a car before. I took the bus, walked, and biked when I was in college. We had a car service, taxis, and the subway in New York City.

Brandon grabbed my car keys from the dining room table.

"What are you doing?" I asked.

"Getting your car keys," said Brandon. He genuinely looked confused by my question.

"Unh, huh. It's my car. I'm driving," I said.

"You don't know where the houses are," replied Brandon.

"I have GPS. Or, if you want, you can navigate old school. But I am driving."

Brandon knew I was serious. He immediately tossed me the car keys. Antonio was giggling.

"Okay, let's go," I said as I grabbed my purse and sunglasses.

Brandon and Antonio followed me out of the suite and to the Lusso parking lot. I had parked in a corner away from all other cars.

"I don't know why you didn't valet park," said Brandon. He was about to complain about the walk across the parking lot.

"I didn't want my new car to get scratched," I said.

Brandon shook his head.

"They wouldn't have scratched your car. I've never had a car scratched by the valets here."

"Okay. I didn't want anyone else driving the car just yet," I said.

Brandon wisely decided to drop the subject. Whether there was any sense to my reasoning or not didn't matter.

I climbed in on the driver's side. Brandon got in the passenger side and Antonio sat in back. As soon as I started the car, Antonio opened the rear sun roof. Brandon punched the address to the first house into the GPS and we were off.

The first house we were visiting was only about a ten minute drive from Lusso. As we pulled into the circular driveway, Steve, our real estate agent, was waiting for us by his car. I pulled up behind Steve's car.

"It's beautiful," I said as we got out of the car.

The house was a two-story estate overlooking the Pacific Ocean. Its exterior was beige stucco with a Mediterranean-style tiled roof. A large stone walkway and steps led to the impressive solid wood front door.

"The house was built in 1920, but completely renovated two years ago. It has all its original charm with every modern convenience," said Steve.

As he opened the front door, he continued his sales pitch.

"It is 7,200 square feet with six bedrooms and six and a half bathrooms, chef's kitchen, two eating areas, two living areas, a study, and a game room. But wait until you see the ocean view and the pool."

We stepped into a grand foyer. Cathedral ceilings reached up toward the sky. In front of us, a large staircase led to the second floor. To our left was a formal dining room with a table that comfortably sat twelve. To our right was a formal living room. Beautiful hardwood floors ran throughout the entire first floor.

We crossed through the dining room and into the massive chef's kitchen with top end stainless steel appliances and granite counter tops. There was a spacious breakfast nook that overlooked the backyard. The kitchen opened into a family room.

The family room had the same cathedral ceilings as the entry to the house. A large stone fireplace anchored the room. French doors opened onto a large stone patio with a sweeping view of the ocean. One end of the patio had an outdoor kitchen for grilling.

The stone steps of the patio led to a lush green lawn that was wonderfully landscaped. Antonio's eyes grew wide as he surveyed the glistening water of the swimming pool at the end of the yard.

"Wow," he said with a broad smile.

"Let's take a look at the upstairs," said Steve.

We followed him back into the house and up the stairs. There were four large bedrooms, each with its own private bathroom. They all had ocean views.

The master bedroom was a true master retreat. It had a sitting area that was as big as many living rooms. The en suite bathroom was as elegant as the Lusso. A bonus for me were the two, large, walk-in closets. French doors opened onto a private balcony that overlooked the backyard and spectacular view of the Pacific Ocean.

"So, what do you think?" asked Steve.

"I absolutely love it," I said.

"Awesome," offered Antonio. "I already know which room I want."

"Any room other than this one," said Brandon. "This would be for Ashley and me. But we are getting ahead of ourselves. What's the list price?"

"Nine million five hundred thousand," answered Steve.

"Is that market value?" asked Brandon.

"Actually a little below market value. The sellers are motivated. They are moving to Europe and would prefer to get the house sold before they leave," said Steve.

"I like it very much. But we should probably look at the other two houses before we make a decision," said Brandon.

"Fair enough. Why don't you take another walk through the house and then we can head over to the next house," said Steve.

We did another walk through the house and around the backyard again. We followed Steve and toured the other two houses. They were also very nice. But I was in love with the first house.

"Well?" asked Brandon when we were back in my car.

"The second and third houses were both very nice. But I absolutely loved the first one," I said.

"Me, too. I think we could be very happy there. It has a great location and the ocean view is second to none. What do you think, son? Should we buy the first house?"

"Yes!" exclaimed Antonio.

"Well, I guess we have made our decision," said Brandon.

We informed Steve and he got right to work on submitting our offer. A few hours later, we received a call from Steve that the sellers had accepted our offer. We had it conditioned on an inspection, but didn't expect any issues. We made a cash offer, so we could schedule a quick closing. We wanted to be settled into the house before school started for Antonio.

We had just been seated for dinner to celebrate when my cell phone rang. It was Chelsea.

"I'll take it," she said when I answered.

"What?" I asked. My head was full of all the details about buying the house.

"The job at the foundation as legal counsel. I'll take it," she said.

"Oh, Chels, you don't know how happy that makes me. That is the cherry on top of what has been a great day."

I told her about the house.

I had to pinch myself. Not long ago my wedding to Brandon was in question. We had turned a tough corner and everything was looking up. I smiled as I looked across the table at Brandon and Antonio. The two men in my life.

Chapter 27

Our house was controlled chaos the morning of our wedding. Brandon's family, my family, and our wedding party joined us for brunch. Davet, Brandon's personal chef, decided to stay in New York to open his own restaurant, but he agreed to prepare a special brunch for our wedding day.

We had just finished eating and Brandon and Antonio left for Lusso to get ready for the wedding. Brandon's parents left moments later to make sure that all the arrangements were going as planned at Lusso. His mother and my mother had been glued to each other's sides at lunch talking animatedly about last-minute details.

As much as I loved Hunter's parents, I was glad that they would keep him company before the ceremony. And I was sure that they wanted plenty of last minute photographs before Hunter became a married man.

My mother, sister, Chelsea, and Maria were helping me get ready at the house. Chelsea helped me into the dress and then zipped up the back for me. Then she returned to the others so that I could make a grand entrance. I stepped out of my walk-in closet into the master bedroom. Everyone turned to face me.

"You look so beautiful, dear," said my mother with tears in her eyes.

"Brandon is one lucky guy," commented my sister.

"Ash, I know I was with you when you bought it, but you are stunning in that dress," said Chelsea.

"Turn around, let us see the back," said Maria.

I twirled. I felt like a princess. A princess on her wedding day. And I was marrying my prince charming.

Our wedding photographer snapped some pictures. He and his assistant had been with us all morning. We wanted to capture every moment of our wedding day. His assistant had left with Brandon and Antonio to get pictures of them as they got ready at Lusso.

There was a knock at the bedroom door. Chelsea opened the door and my father was in the hallway.

"The limos are here," he announced.

We all made our way downstairs. We had a car for my parents, my bridesmaids, and a white Rolls Royce limousine for me. My parents' car pulled out of the driveway and our car followed for the ten minute drive to Lusso.

When we arrived, Lusso's wedding planner greeted us. My mother went ahead to meet with Brandon's mother for their entrance. The wedding planner took my dad, Chelsea, my bridesmaids, and me to the bride's room to wait before the start of the ceremony.

It was a beautiful autumn day with a warm, gentle breeze coming off the Pacific Ocean. Brandon and I had decided to get married outside on Lusso's expansive lawn that overlooked the ocean.

I peeked out to see the start of the ceremony. I watched Brandon's mother walk down the aisle to begin the ceremony. She was followed by the groomsmen, Brandon's best man, and then Brandon. I had to catch my breath. Brandon was so handsome and regal looking.

He was dressed in a classic black tuxedo. It was tailored perfectly to his athletic and muscular frame. His face looked even more handsome than the day we first met. That day a little over four years ago seemed so distant. We had been through so much and soon we would be husband and wife.

"Okay, ladies. Time to go," said the wedding planner.

My bridesmaids made their way down the aisle. They were wearing a one shoulder satin dress in Midnight blue. They looked beautiful. Especially my younger sister. Chelsea followed the bridesmaids down the aisle and looked stunning in the dress.

"You look so beautiful," Antonio said to me as the wedding planner placed him in the processional just ahead of me.

"Thank you, sweetie. And you are so handsome."

Antonio was wearing a tuxedo that matched the groomsmen. He was our ring bearer and proudly showed me the rings on the pillow. As Antonio made his way down the aisle, my father took my the arm.

"Are you ready, dear?" he asked.

I took a deep breath.

"Yes. I have never been more ready for anything in my life," I said.

I saw my dad wipe a tear from the corner of his eye.

"I can't believe that my little girl is getting married. I love you, pumpkin."

"Stop. You are going to make me cry," I said.

"I just want you to know how much your mother and I love you."

"All set?" asked the wedding planner.

I nodded my head. My dad and I made our way down the aisle as the orchestra played Pachelbel Canon in D. When we reached the front, I took my place next to Brandon.

The minister smiled at us and then began.

"Dearly beloved: We have come together to witness the joining together of this man and this woman in Matrimony. The union of husband and wife in heart, body, and mind is intended for their mutual joy; for the help and comfort given one another in prosperity and adversity. Therefore marriage is not to be entered into unadvisedly or lightly, but reverently, deliberately, and in accordance with the purposes for which it was intended."

The minister then looked out onto the guests gathered.

"Into this union, Brandon Mitchell and Ashley Sullivan now come to be joined. If any of you can show just cause why they may not lawfully be married, speak now; or else forever hold your peace."

He waited for what seemed an eternity. I guess he really wanted to be sure that no one had any objections. Then he looked at Brandon and me.

"I require and charge you both, that if either of you know any reason why you may not be united in marriage lawfully, you do now confess it."

Been there and done that, I thought. Granted, Gina had orchestrated erasing Brandon's annulment to her, but at least we had taken care of that issue.

The minister looked at me with his kind and warm eyes.

"Ashley, will you have this man to be your husband; to live together in the covenant of marriage? Will you love him, comfort him, honor and keep him, in sickness and in health; and, forsaking all others, be faithful to him as long as you both shall live?"

"I will," I replied.

The minister then looked at Brandon.

"Brandon, will you have this woman to be your wife; to live together in the covenant of marriage? Will you love her, comfort her, honor and keep her, in sickness and in health; and, forsaking all others, be faithful to her as long as you both shall live?"

"I will," replied Brandon.

"Will all of you witnessing these promises do all in your power to uphold these two persons in their marriage?" asked the minister to our gathered guests.

"We will," our guests responded.

"Now for the exchanging of vows," said the minister.

Brandon and I faced each other and Brandon took my right hand in his.

"I, Brandon, take you, Ashley, to be my wife, to have and to hold from this day forward, for better for worse, for richer for poorer, in sickness and in health, to love and to cherish, until we are parted by death. This is my solemn vow."

Then we loosed our hands. I took Brandon's right hand in mine.

"I, Ashley, take you, Brandon, to be my husband, to have and to hold from this day forward, for better for worse, for richer for poorer, in sickness and in health, to love and to cherish, until we are parted by death. This is my solemn vow."

The minister nodded to Antonio and he stepped forward. Brandon's best man took our rings off of the pillow and handed them to the minister. The minister handed my ring to Brandon.

Brandon placed the ring on my ring-finger.

"Ashley, I give you this ring as a symbol of my vow, and with all that I am, and all that I have, I honor you."

The minister then handed me Brandon's ring. I placed the ring on his ring-finger.

"Brandon, I give you this ring as a symbol of my vow, and with all that I am, and all that I have, I honor you."

"Now that Brandon and Ashley have given themselves to each other by solemn vows, with the joining of hands and the giving and receiving of a ring, I pronounce that they are husband and wife."

Brandon and I kissed as our guests applauded. It was our most sensual kiss. Our first kiss as husband and wife.

Chapter 28

"Okay, be a good boy," Brandon said to Antonio.

"I will."

Brandon's parents had agreed to stay at our house with Antonio while we were on our honeymoon. Gina came to our house regularly to spend time with Antonio. That arrangement was working out well.

Frankly, I think Gina preferred it that way. She had never been much of a mother to Antonio. Her attempt to take him away was more about getting at Brandon. She was actually happy with her job at *Jacqueline* and enjoyed living in Santa Barbara. So far, so good.

"Have a wonderful time," Brandon's mother said to us.

"Don't worry about a thing. We plan on spoiling our grandson and having a great time doing it," said Brandon's dad.

"Right. Like he's not spoiled enough already," said Brandon.

"It is the grandparents' prerogative to spoil their grandchild," Brandon's dad replied.

"I left Antonio's school schedule on the fridge. We have already contacted Santa Barbara Academy and informed them that you will be dropping him off and picking him up while we are away. He has a week's worth of school uniforms cleaned and pressed hanging in his closet," I said.

"Our bags are in the car. I just got word that the jet is ready to go when we arrive at the airport," said Brandon.

I hugged Brandon's parents and Antonio.

"I love you. Be good," I said to Antonio.

"I love you, too," he said.

I thought that I was going to cry. I never tired of hearing Antonio telling me that he loved me. I knew that I was his step mom, but I didn't love him any less than if he had been my own son.

"Okay. We will see you next week," I said. I grabbed my purse and headed for the door.

"Ashley, dear. Aren't you forgetting something?" asked Brandon.

"I don't think so," I replied.

"Your car keys? I don't think my parents know how to hotwire a car."

"Oh, right." I dug my car keys out of my purse and handed them to Brandon's dad.

Okay, so I was still a little protective of my car. But I honestly had forgotten that the keys were in my purse.

Brandon's parents and Antonio waved goodbye to us as we got into the Aston Martin and left for the airport.

"I'm excited about our honeymoon in Paris, but I already miss Antonio," I said as we pulled out of the driveway.

"I know. But think about all the fun we are going to have." Brandon raised his eyebrows and gave me a seductive smile.

Chapter 29

Four years ago, Brandon swept me off my feet and to Paris for a romantic getaway. It was a vacation to reestablish our relationship. His attempt to win me back after we had broken up. Obviously, it worked.

We had returned to Paris one other time on vacation. For both of our visits we stayed at the Le Bristol Hotel, one of Paris's finest 5-star hotels. We chose Le Bristol for our honeymoon as well.

"Bonjour. Bienvenue sur le Le Bristol," said the desk clerk.

"Bonjour. Mr. and Mrs. Brandon Mitchell," said Brandon.

"Ah, yes. I see that you have the Honeymoon Suite. Congratulations," said the desk clerk.

"Yes. And we added the second bedroom," said Brandon.

"Yes, Mr. Mitchell. It has a fabulous view of the Eiffel Tower."

As we checked in, we were greeted by Le Bristol's adorable Birman cat, Fa-ron.

"Hello, Fa-ron," I said as I reached down and petted his head. "Long time no see."

Close behind Fa-ron was a second Birman feline.

"Who is your friend?" I asked Fa-ron.

"That is Kléopatre," said the desk clerk. "Fa-ron's new girlfriend."

"She is beautiful," I said as I bent down to pet her.

"She is a wonderful cat. Loving, affectionate, playful and delicate," said the desk clerk. "Fa-ron immediately took to her when she joined us this past summer."

From our prior visits, it was clear that Fa-ron never lacked for attention when he wanted it. Still, it was nice that he had a feline friend. Brandon and I finished checking in.

"Congratulations again. Enjoy your stay, Mr. and Mrs. Mitchell," said the desk clerk.

"Thank you," we said.

The bellhop took our bags and we headed to the Honeymoon Suite.

The Honeymoon Suite was located on the eighth and top floor of Le Bristol. Brandon carried me across the threshold. As we entered, I took in how breathtaking the Honeymoon Suite was. It overlooked the highly fashionable rue du Faubourg Saint-Honoré, with a panoramic view over Paris's most beautiful monuments. It had a sloping ceiling and featured a magnificent oak parquet floor with a chevron pattern.

The Honeymoon Suite, in actuality, was more like an elegant apartment. It was more than 2,500 square feet. It had an enormous sitting room, an elegant bedroom with two dressing areas, and a connecting bathroom with a steam shower and spacious bath. The suite was filled with natural light. We also rented the connected second bedroom for its view of the Eiffel Tower.

Brandon tipped the bellhop. After the bellhop left, Brandon took me into his arms. We kissed. Our lips were soft and our breaths warm. Brandon's strong arms held me close as he carried me to the bedroom with a view of the Eiffel Tower.

Chapter 30

On the first full day of our honeymoon we headed to the Pont des Arts bridge. Pont des Arts had long been known as the "Lover's Bridge." It was said that if you shared a kiss on the bridge that your love would last forever. A new tradition had been added to that. Now couples left a lock on the fence of the bridge with a love note before tossing the key into the Seine. The act was supposed to seal a couple's love forever.

Brandon and I had shared both traditions.

"Well, I guess it worked," I said as Brandon and I walked arm-in-arm. "Do you think we can find it?"

"Our lock? I don't know. They probably have to remove them when the fence gets full. To make room for new locks."

"Oh, that would be a bummer. They are supposed to be symbols of eternal love," I said.

"They are. But the fence can only hold so many locks. They need to make sure that all the other tourists who want to place a symbol of their eternal love can do so."

"I guess," I said. "Let's not even look, then. I'd like to think that it is still there. If we don't look, I can't possibly be disappointed."

"Okay. Besides, we are wearing an even more important symbol of our eternal love."

Brandon held up our left hands. We gazed at our wedding rings. We kissed. I had never felt so happy in all my life.

We enjoyed the remainder of our week in Paris. As magical a honeymoon as it was, I was happy to be getting home to Antonio.

"I have really missed him," I said as Brandon and I drove home from the Santa Barbara airport.

"Yeah, me too. He is a great kid."

"Next vacation needs to be a family vacation. Ooh, I know. We should take Antonio to Disney," I said.

"That sounds great. Let's plan that for his next school vacation."

"Yes. That will be so much fun."

I was thrilled to see our house as we pulled into the driveway. Antonio rushed out the front door to greet us.

"What did you bring me from Paris?" he asked as he jumped up into Brandon's arms.

"Hold on there. No, 'hi Dad, how was the honeymoon?'"

"Hi, Dad. How was the honeymoon?" said Antonio with a smile.

"It was wonderful. And you will have to wait just a while to see what we brought you from Paris. We have gifts for you and for Grandma and Grandpa," Brandon said.

Brandon put Antonio back on his feet on the ground. Antonio turned to me and gave me a giant hug.

"I missed you and Dad," he said.

"We missed you too. Did you have a fun time with Grandma and Grandpa?"

"Yes. We swam a lot in the pool. And I had them take me bowling."

Brandon let out a huge laugh.

"Bowling? I would love to have seen that. I don't think my parents had even seen the inside of a bowling alley."

"Hey, we didn't do too badly," said Brandon's dad as he walked down the front steps. "How was the honeymoon?"

"Magical," I said.

"Excellent. Honeymoons should be magical."

"How was your week?" Brandon asked his dad.

"We had a great time. Spoiled our grandson rotten, just like I said we would," his dad replied with a broad smile.

"Of course. It is, after all, grandparents' prerogative," replied Brandon.

"Exactly. Now, your mother fixed us some lunch out on the back patio. We want to hear all about Paris."

"We'll be right there," said Brandon.

Brandon's dad turned and headed back into the house. Antonio took Brandon and me by the hand.

"Come on, let's go," Antonio said as he pulled for us to follow him.

I couldn't believe the life that I had. Four years ago Brandon Mitchell swept me off my feet and I fell head over heels in love. I know it sounds cliché, but it's wonderfully true. There may have been some bumps along the way, but I wouldn't trade what I had for anything. I was married to the man of my dreams and we had a wonderful family. We couldn't be any happier.

As we reached the front door, Brandon's cell phone buzzed. He pulled his phone out of his pocket. He checked the screen.

"Santa Barbara Police. I should get this," Brandon said.

He answered. I could tell by the look on his face that it was bad news. After a moment he thanked the police officer on the other end of the phone and told them that he would be right over.

"Antonio, why don't you run along ahead and help Grandma and Grandpa. I need to go check on something at work. I'm afraid that it can't wait. But Ashley will join you and Grandma and Grandpa in a minute."

"Okay. I'll save you something to eat," replied Antonio as he bounded up the steps and through the front door.

"What's wrong at work?" I asked.

"Nothing. I didn't want to upset Antonio until we know what is going on. Gina was found passed out in her townhouse. The police and paramedics are there now. They found some empty pill bottles. They don't know what she took or how bad it is."

"Oh my gosh! I know Gina is not our favorite person, but . . ."

"I know."

"Oh, and poor Antonio."

"That's why we can't say anything to him until we know what we are dealing with. I'm going to head over now. I'll call you once I know something. We'll figure out what to do from there," said Brandon.

I nodded my head. I kissed Brandon on the cheek. He got into his car and I watched him drive away. I thought about all we had been through recently. I thought about how Gina Arlotti had turned our lives upside down in both troubling and wonderful ways.

I thought about how things seemed like they were working out for Gina. She liked the position Brandon established for her at *Jacqueline*. Gina actually seemed happy. Everything seemed to be great for all of us. Now all I could do was think about the tragic call from the police and wonder what we might learn next.

Chapter 31

Brandon had called me from the hospital with an update on Gina's condition. She had overdosed on sleeping pills. Thankfully, the paramedics who had arrived on the scene worked quickly. They were credited with saving her life. The ER team at the hospital made certain that no trace of the pills remained in her system and that her condition was stable.

Brandon called again to let me know that Gina had been transferred to a room and was under careful watch. It was still uncertain whether the overdose was accidental or not, but it didn't look good. Brandon said he was on his way home. It had been twenty minutes since his last call, so I expected him any moment.

I sat in the living room with Brandon's parents. Antonio was already in bed and asleep. He thought that Brandon just needed to go into the office and was working late. I had no idea what we were going to tell him about Gina.

The front door signal from our alarm system beeped that the door was open.

"That must be Brandon," I said to his parents.

A moment later Brandon walked into the living room and sat down beside me on the couch.

"You look exhausted," said Brandon's mother.

"Well, I certainly wasn't expecting to spend the evening in the hospital waiting room," he replied. "Is Antonio already in bed?"

"Yes," I answered. "I checked on him a little while ago. He is sound asleep."

"Good," Brandon said. Then he continued.

"I'm not sure that we know much more than what I told you on the phone. Gina is out of the woods as far as the overdose being life threatening. The doctors don't believe there is any permanent damage, but they are running tests."

"Do they think that she may have overdosed on purpose? She didn't seem to be giving any signs that she was unhappy," I said.

"She had dinner plans with a neighbor, so she seemed to be deliberate in drinking the wine and taking the pills before dinner," said Brandon.

"That doesn't sound good," said Brandon's dad.

"I agree. It doesn't make sense that she would take sleeping pills before going out to dinner. Especially combining the pills with alcohol," said Brandon.

"I feel terrible," I said.

"It certainly is concerning," said Brandon.

"Yes, I feel terrible that this has happened," I said, "but I'm troubled that all the recent changes are a contributing factor."

"Ashley, you can't blame this on the custody situation or her and Antonio moving to Santa Barbara," said Brandon.

"But they could be factors," I said.

"I'm not saying that recent events are not possible factors. What I am saying is that we can't blame ourselves for this. It is not our fault," said Brandon.

"I agree with Brandon," said Brandon's mom. "Ashley, dear, you and Brandon can't blame yourselves. You are both doing such a wonderful job with Antonio. He is happy. Brandon gave Gina a good job, one that she seemed very happy with."

"Yes," said Brandon's dad, "there must be other, more significant, factors at work."

"The truth is, we don't know that much about Gina's history. There could be any number of things going on," said Brandon.

"Do you remember Gina mentioning that she is estranged from her parents?" I asked.

"Yes. I remember her telling us that Antonio has never even met them," said Brandon. "But she has been estranged from them for more than ten years. Why would that suddenly be relevant?"

"I don't know. I'm just thinking out loud about aspects of her life that are out of the norm," I replied.

"Maybe she received some news from them, or about them that upset her?" mentioned Brandon's mom.

"All of this is just wild speculation on our part. But I do believe that we need to find out as much as we can. Gina is certainly not my favorite person in the world. However, she is Antonio's mother. We need for her to be as healthy and happy as possible for him," said Brandon.

"Well, we certainly should speak with Gina when she is alert. But I don't know how much she will tell us about what is going on. Maybe she isn't fully aware herself," I said.

"What do you think we should do?" asked Brandon.

"Why don't we hire Galletta Detective Agency to look more into Gina's background? Maybe there are some pieces of the puzzle that we can put together to get a clearer picture," I suggested.

"That's a good idea. I'll call them in the morning," said Brandon.

"We also need to decide how much we are going to tell Antonio," I said.

"Well, I don't think we can keep this from him," said Brandon.

"No. I think we should tell him that Gina is in the hospital. But it is important that we reassure him that she is not in any immediate danger," I said.

"Agreed. I think we tell him just enough to be honest, but as few details as possible. It is hard enough for us to figure out," replied Brandon.

I wasn't sure that I felt much better about the situation, but I was thankful that Gina was medically stable and under watchful care. We also had the beginnings of a plan to deal with the situation. That was something. I only hoped that what developed would not be more than we could handle.

Chapter 32

Brandon and I explained to Antonio that his mother was not feeling well and needed to spend a few days in the hospital. We received an update from her doctors that she was now alert and could receive visitors. Brandon told Antonio that we would visit Gina during visiting hours after school.

Antonio never ceases to amaze me. He is a bright and mature ten. He was naturally upset at his mother being in the hospital, but took it well. Brandon and I did our best to reassure him that she was okay and he seemed to accept that.

"Have a good day," said Brandon as we pulled to a stop at the drop off spot at Santa Barbara Academy.

"Don't forget that we are going to see mom in the hospital later," Antonio said as he hopped out the back of my car.

"We won't," I said. "Love you."

"Love you, son," said Brandon.

"Love you guys too. See you later." Antonio closed the back door, pulled his backpack straps over his shoulders. We watched him happily walk into the school.

"I am so glad that he has school to help take his mind off of Gina," I said.

"Me too. But he has taken it well," replied Brandon.

"I think we explained it well to him. I guess we are not so bad at this parenting thing," I said.

"I just wish we could figure Gina out. She's clearly troubled," Brandon said.

"Once we get some information from Matteo Silvi, we'll have more to go on," I said.

Matteo Silvi was the private investigator that we worked with in Milan, Italy to locate Gina and Antonio when she disappeared with him. Brandon and I hoped that Matteo would uncover something useful that might give us a better understanding of Gina's behavior. Maybe then we could be of more help.

I pulled my car forward and exited the school parking lot. I knew that Brandon preferred to drive, but I loved driving my car so much. Brandon flipped through e-mails on his phone and tapped his foot.

"Do you have to do that?" I asked.

"Do what? I'm just checking my e-mail."

"No. Tap your foot like that. It's like you are trying to keep time to a private drum beat in your head."

"Does it bother you?"

"A little."

"Sorry. Nervous energy."

"Is it your way of telling me how much you hate not driving?"

"Not on purpose. It's a subconscious thing."

"Well, deal with it. You know the rule. If we take my car, I drive. She's my baby. Besides, we are a modern couple. The woman can drive."

"Never said you couldn't."

"That's because you don't have a choice."

"That too."

Brandon's face hardened.

"What's wrong?" I asked.

"It's probably nothing, but some of the board members are bitching again about the *Adele* acquisition."

"Seriously? It hasn't been that long. They need to give it time. It will be good in the long run."

"They are not very long run thinkers. Ever since Davenport Media went public, all they have cared about is our stock price."

"Well, the company has been doing very well over that time. The top fashion magazine that has been very profitable. I don't know what they are so concerned about."

"They are concerned that we spent a lot of cash when we bought *Adele*."

"Don't they understand that adage of needing to spend money to make money?" I asked.

"Only if it improves the stock price and shareholder profits. The *Adele* acquisition has yet to do that."

"It has only been a few months. Are they really that shortsighted?"

"Shortsighted enough to cause some major headaches."

"Well, you and your grandmother are the largest shareholders in the company. If you two are satisfied with earnings, I don't know why they have their panties all in a bunch."

That actually got a chuckle out of Brandon.

"I don't think a bunch of old guys wear panties. At least they don't seem the type," Brandon said with a laugh.

"Just an expression. But, hey, you never know what some of them may be into."

"I'd rather not even think about that." Brandon sighed.

"I've read about all I can take at the moment," he announced as he put his phone into sleep mode.

"I'm sure it will all work out."

I tried to sound reassuring. I'm not sure that I was all that convincing. We both knew that the Davenport Media Board of Directors were a bunch of hard asses. Brandon rarely fretted over much. The fact that reading the e-mails bothered him that much was concerning.

I hated to see him worrying. But even worried he was still the most handsome and charming man I knew. In fact, I thought that he should be awarded Most Handsome Man Alive every year.

"Hey, slow down lead foot," said Brandon.

"Oops. Sorry." I let my foot up off the gas pedal.

"What are your plans for the rest of the day?" asked Brandon.

"I have a lunch meeting with Chelsea. Then we are meeting with the faculty at Davenport School of the Arts."

"I miss having you at the office, but I am glad that you decided to devote your time to starting the foundation."

"Me too. I'm very excited. I think that we can raise a lot of money and attention for our charitable efforts. It will also be fun working with Chelsea."

I was so happy when Chelsea agreed to work for the Mitchell Family Foundation as our legal counsel. I couldn't imagine anyone better in that role. She had been instrumental in handling all the legal aspects of establishing the foundation. We were now ready to roll up our sleeves and raise funds to support our charitable causes.

I dropped Brandon off at our house to get his car. He was heading to our new Santa Barbara office and I was driving his parents to the airport for their flight back to New York.

"Have a good day," I said to Brandon.

"I'll try. Say hi to Chelsea for me."

"I will."

We kissed and then Brandon hopped in his Aston Martin and sped off to the office.

"And he thinks I have a lead foot?" I said to myself.

"Penny for your thoughts?" asked Brandon's mother as she came out the front door with her luggage.

"Oh, nothing," I said.

"Well, it is nice to see a smile on that pretty face of yours. It has been a trying twenty-four hours."

Brandon's father followed his wife out of the house and closed the front door behind him. He pulled his suitcase behind him over to the trunk of my car.

"Thanks for giving us a ride to the airport," he said. "We could have called a car service."

"Nonsense. I'm happy to take you. I don't have to be anywhere until lunch."

We put their bags into the trunk.

"But someone needs to sit up front with me. I don't want to feel like a chauffeur," I said teasingly.

"I call shotgun," said Brandon's mother.

For billionaires, they were very down to earth. I was fortunate to have the in-laws that I did. I truly loved them. And I enjoyed their company. Although I guess now I was, technically, a billionaire myself, and I'm still pretty down to earth.

We hopped in my car and I took my in-laws to the airport. I swung by the gym and was able to make an aerobics class. I showered, dressed, and headed to meet Chelsea for lunch. It was mostly a business lunch, but I still wanted to hear her dish about her new boyfriend. So, a little lunch, a little work, and a little girl talk with my BFF. Not a bad way to spend an afternoon.

Chapter 33

Chelsea and I met at a little beachfront café not far from Santa Barbara University. We sat on the outside patio overlooking the water. Between going to Italy and my honeymoon, apart from my wedding, I hadn't seen Chelsea much the past month. That was unusual for us, so I was really looking forward to getting details on her dating life.

"I love the fried clams here," said Chelsea as she looked over the menu.

"They are good. But how can you not get the lobster? Besides, lunch is on me."

"Very tempting. Okay, I'll order the lobster."

When the waiter arrived, we ordered two of the lobster specials.

"How is Gina doing?" Chelsea asked.

I had called Chelsea about what happened. I had updated her with a few text messages and told her I would fill her in at lunch.

"Better. Medically she is stable and alert. Brandon and I will take Antonio to visit tonight."

"How is Antonio handling it?"

"Naturally he was upset about his mom being in the hospital, but he is taking it very well. We did our best to reassure him that she will be okay. He's a great kid. And he is definitely Brandon's son. Very little seems to rattle him."

"Still no idea what really happened with Gina?"

"No. We have the investigator in Milan gathering whatever he can find. See if there is any information that may help explain what is going on."

"So you don't think that Gina would be honest with you at this point?"

"I don't know. But I'm not sure it's so much that as she isn't entirely clear about what is going on."

"I hope you guys learn something of value. I don't particularly like nor trust Gina Arlotti, but I don't want any harm to come to her. I especially don't want to see that sweet little boy hurt."

"That's basically the plan. Learn what we can. Hope it is enough to help Gina. Make sure Antonio is protected no matter what."

"You're a great Step Mom. Frankly, you're more like a full mother than Gina probably ever has been."

"Thanks. But Brandon and I are just sort of figuring parenting out as we go along. It helps that Antonio is an easy kid to parent."

"It's amazing how much has changed. The last time we lived in Santa Barbara we were recent college graduates. Brandon was your 'Mr. Handsome CEO' celebrity crush. Now look at you. Ashley Mitchell. Married to the man of your dreams, heading your own charitable foundation, a step-mom . . . It suits you," said Chelsea.

"Well, one thing is exactly the same as it has been since our freshman year of college. You are still my very best friend in the entire world."

We clinked our glasses in a toast to our friendship.

"Now, speaking of celebrity crushes . . . tell me what is going on with your beautiful NFL quarterback," I said.

Chelsea had met Ethan Bennett, a Super Bowl winning quarterback, at a Caribbean resort during the winter break of our senior year in college. Chelsea and I had saved up our money for a year for a girl's tropical getaway. Chelsea and Ethan really hit it off, but they lived very different lives at the time. So that was pretty much it until a few weeks ago when Ethan called Chelsea.

"There really isn't much to tell just yet," said Chelsea. Then she smiled. A playful grin. Then she continued. "Other than he is totally amazing."

"Chels, that is great."

"Well, now that we are both in the same city and neither of us is dating anyone seriously, we figured we should give it a try."

Ethan had been traded from his former team – a team that he led to two Super Bowl titles in five years – after being hurt and missing most of last season. He was now the starting quarterback for the Santa Barbara Bobcats.

"Brandon still scratches his head at how any team could trade Ethan Bennett. At least as a football fan. He said it probably made business sense. I don't understand any of it. Trades, draft picks . . . whatever," I said.

"I'm with you. Until Ethan, the only thing I paid attention to was how cute some of the player's butts looked in their uniforms," said Chelsea.

"Like Ethan's," I teased.

"Yes. Definitely."

"I agree. But let's not get sidetracked. Get me caught up. We haven't been able to talk details. Come on, give it up," I said.

"Okay. Okay. Be patient."

"I don't recall patience being something you had much of when you wanted to know about me and Brandon."

"Fair enough."

The waiter came with our lobster specials. He refilled our drink glasses.

"I love how they pull the lobster meat out for you," said Chelsea.

"Makes it easier and much less messy, but I think it takes some of the fun out of it. Part of the experience is working the shell to get to the meat," I said.

Chelsea simply shrugged her shoulders as she dipped a piece of lobster in melted butter and popped it into her mouth. She closed her eyes and savored the taste. She had a look of pure satisfaction on her face.

"The lobster here is fabulous," I said. "Alright, tell me about Ethan."

"You know that he and I kept in touch after our vacation in college. But with his playing in a different city from where I lived, his travel with the team, and my going to law school, we just couldn't find enough time to make a go of dating each other."

"Chels, I know all of that. Fast forward to present day, please."

"You are not normally so impatient," said Chelsea.

"It's because this is the first time that you have had a guy that might turn out to be a lasting relationship."

"This is true. Ethan could be a keeper," said Chelsea. "Okay, so as soon as he knew he was being traded . . ."

"I know that part, too. Chels, skip ahead."

"Ash, I like summarizing. It helps me to tell the story."

I don't know why I was so impatient. I guess I just needed to hear some good news. I also wanted the juicy details of Chelsea's recent dates with Ethan.

"May I continue? Uninterrupted this time?" said Chelsea.

"Yes. Sorry. Go ahead."

I decided to eat my lobster and let Chelsea recount her brief history with Ethan however she wanted to.

"Okay. Now, where was I?"

"Ethan called when he knew he was being traded," I said.

"Oh, right. Ethan called me when he found out he was being traded to the Santa Barbara Bobcats. I had e-mailed him that I was moving back to Santa Barbara to work for the foundation. He called and asked if I was dating anyone. I told him that I was not. He asked if I was interested in getting together. Naturally, I said yes," she said.

I didn't say anything. I just ate and listened. I was still waiting for her to get to more recent events. Chelsea continued to recount, which was all review for me, how she and Ethan went on a few dates early in the fall.

She reminded me how she had wanted Ethan to be her date to my wedding, but he had an away game that weekend and couldn't make it. She was finally getting up to the prior week. Brandon and I were on our honeymoon in Paris. That was the missing week of Chelsea and Ethan that I was waiting for.

"While you and Brandon were on your honeymoon, Ethan and I were creating some of our own magic here," Chelsea said.

"Finally," I said. Okay, I had been patient enough. Chelsea just gave me a playful grin.

"Wait a minute," I said, "you were doing all that on purpose just to make me wait. Chels, you were messing with me."

"Well, . . . maybe a little," she said.

I flicked my napkin at her playfully. I also had a broad smile. Lunch with Chelsea was the first time that I had smiled or laughed since we got the news about Gina.

"Enough already. You've had your fun. Now tell me about last week," I said. I was about ready to jump out of my seat with anticipation.

"The Bobcats had a bye week last weekend . . ."

"A what?" I asked.

"Bye week. It is a week when they don't have a game. Every team gets a bye week one week during the season," Chelsea replied.

"Oh. Why do they do that?"

"Do you really care?"

"Not if it delays my hearing about you and Ethan," I replied.

"Ethan still had practices and watching film to prepare for their next game, but a lighter schedule and more time off. Good news for me. It gave us some quality time together. We had some romantic dinners. He took me out on his boat and we drove to wine country for tasting and dinner," she said.

"Ooh, that sounds romantic," I said.

"It was. Like something out of a romance novel."

"So, you really like him? There is an emotional connection?" I asked.

"Yes. I truly enjoy spending time with him. We have a lot in common. He is smart, fun, easy to talk to. I really want to make it work with him. I'm even enjoying learning all about football," she said.

"Wow, you must really like him. Chels, I am so happy for you. I've been waiting for you to meet a guy that you felt a connection with."

I got up and went over and gave her a big hug. It seemed that Chelsea was finding the type of relationship that I found with Brandon. I hoped that was true. Chelsea deserved that love in her life.

"Oh, I almost forgot to mention. Ethan has tickets for us for next weekend's game. We can take Brandon and Antonio. They are in the owner's luxury box," she said.

"That sounds like fun. Brandon will be very excited. I think Antonio will too. He is a soccer player, which is football everywhere else in the world, but he also loves baseball and has been getting into American football."

"Ethan has also arranged for a private, behind-the-scenes, tour of the stadium and to meet the other players and coaches after one of their practices. I just need to arrange a day with him."

"That is very nice of him. I don't know any ten-year-old boy who wouldn't get excited about such an opportunity," I said.

"Probably thirty-three-year-old boys as well," Chelsea said.

"True. I don't know who will be more excited, Antonio or Brandon."

We finished our lunch and did, eventually, get around to discussing foundation business. We then left to meet with the president of Santa Barbara University and the dean of the Davenport School of the Arts at the University.

It felt a little strange being back on campus and meeting with the president and dean in our roles as executive director and legal counsel of the Mitchell Family Foundation. But I was thrilled to be in the position that I was to give back to the university and the arts program that meant so much to me.

After our meeting at the university, I said goodbye to Chelsea in the parking lot of the administration building.

"I think that went very well," I said.

"Me too. Very productive," said Chelsea.

"I'll talk to you tomorrow," I said. "I need to run and pick Antonio up from school."

"Say hello to the little cutie for me," said Chelsea.

"That will make his day," I said.

Antonio had a little crush on Chelsea. Ten-year-old girls might be icky to him, but a twenty-six-year-old with supermodel looks was an entirely different matter. Boys and men of all ages had crushes on Chelsea Richards.

I picked Antonio up from school. He seemed in a good mood, but asked immediately about visiting Gina in the hospital. I told him that we would go during visiting hours after dinner. When we arrived home, Brandon's car was already in the garage. I thought it strange that he would be home so early.

Antonio and I entered the house and Brandon was in the family room drinking a beer and watching Sports Center. He still had his suit on, but he had removed his tie and unbuttoned the top button of his shirt. Brandon turned his head as Antonio and I walked into the room. Brandon tried to hide it, but there was a look of dire concern on his face.

Chapter 34

"Hi, dad," said Antonio as he jumped into Brandon's lap.

Brandon kissed Antonio on the cheek.

"How was school today?" Brandon asked Antonio.

"Good. We got to play flag football in PE. I caught a touchdown!" said Antonio.

"That's awesome. Did you learn anything interesting in class?"

"No. I like PE best."

"Why don't you go upstairs to your room and change out of your school uniform," Brandon told him.

"Okay. Ashley said we are going to see mom in the hospital after dinner."

"Yes. We'll eat a little early tonight, then go for a visit," Brandon replied.

Antonio hopped off Brandon's lap. He grabbed his backpack and headed upstairs. I waited until Antonio was out of the room, then I sat next to Brandon on the couch.

"You're home early and I didn't like the look on your face when we walked in," I said.

"You could tell, huh?"

"Brandon, at this point I know you better than you know yourself. What's wrong?"

"More shit with the board of directors. It seems that they are lining up against me in greater numbers. More members are siding with Ron Waters in making noise about the *Adele* acquisition."

Ron Waters was the Chairman of the Davenport Media Board of Directors. He had been a strong supporter of Jacqueline as President and Brandon as CEO. That all changed when they pushed for the *Adele* acquisition. He was cool to the idea. They pushed through the necessary votes on the board to make the acquisition, but trouble started brewing soon after.

In recent weeks, Ronald Waters had gone from an ally to downright hostile toward Jacqueline and, especially, Brandon. There were rumblings that some on the board were considering a takeover of Davenport Media from another company. Something that Jacqueline and Brandon were against.

"I know it is troubling, but your grandmother built the company. Your dad was the first CEO. You took over for him when he retired. This company wouldn't exist or have thrived without your family," I said.

"True. But when we went public a number of years ago, we gave up the control of a privately held, family-owned company. It was the right decision at the time. We needed the capital from selling shares to grow *Jacqueline* magazine," said Brandon.

"I understand all of that. But the board needs to recognize and honor you and your grandmother's wishes."

"Unfortunately, they don't. And if there are enough on the board who vote to sell the company, then we would have to fight by lining up enough shareholders to go against the board."

"Then do that," I said.

"It's not that simple. We hold the largest individual shares of stock, but not the overall majority. That is where the board has power to represent all the other shareholders. We would need to get enough other shareholders to go against the board. Most shareholders only care about the value of the stock. If it is down and the board convinces them that it will go back up by selling the company . . ."

"Then family history doesn't account for much," I said.

"Exactly," said Brandon.

"So what are you going to do?" I asked.

"I'm talking to board members. I'm talking to other major shareholders. I'm seeing if I have enough allies to prevent a sale of the company. Grandmother is doing the same. About all we can do."

"Okay. So what is the worst-case scenario?"

"The company gets sold and the board, most likely, fires me as CEO and my grandmother as President."

I nodded my head in understanding.

"I know how painful that would be for you. It would be especially hard on your grandmother. The company is her legacy. But we would be okay. We would get through it," I said.

"I suppose. It's not like we'd lose absolutely everything. It's not like we don't have a lot of money in the bank and numerous investment portfolios beyond Davenport Media. Financially, we are more than set. It's not about the money. It's about the company that bears my grandmother's name."

"I know." I put my arms around Brandon and hugged him.

I rested my head against his chest. I could hear his heart beating and felt the rhythm of his breathing. I wished that I could make everything better. But I couldn't. If I was honest, my greatest fear wasn't losing the company. It was losing Brandon and Antonio.

I knew that Brandon would be devastated if the company was sold and he lost his position. He would be embarrassed. He would feel like he failed his family and the employees of

Davenport Media. It would change him. And that would change us.

Chapter 35

We arrived at Santa Barbara hospital at the start of visiting hours. We wanted Antonio to have time with Gina, but didn't want to be out late as it was a school night. Brandon had spoken to Gina earlier and they agreed to not cause any concern for Antonio.

We entered Gina's room and she looked up at us from her bed.

"Venite a dare mamma un bacio," she said to Antonio.

"Mamma, in English please," Antonio said. He was very insistent on only speaking English.

Brandon and I discovered his position was common of children who move to the United States from countries that don't speak English as their first language.

"Come give Mommy a kiss," she repeated in English.

Antonio padded over and kissed Gina on the cheek. Then she hugged him.

"I have missed you," she said.

"Are you feeling better?" Antonio asked.

"Yes. They are taking good care of me. How is school?"

"Good. I caught a touchdown in flag football."

"Very good."

"Why don't you tell your mother what we will be doing on Sunday," said Brandon.

"Oh, yeah. Miss Chelsea got us tickets to the football game . . ."

"American football or what they call soccer?" asked Gina.

"American football. I just call it football now. The other I call soccer now."

Antonio wanted to be clear that he was using the same terminology as his friends here in the United States.

Antonio and Gina talked for a while longer. He told her more about school and his friends. Gina seemed genuinely happy to see him. Not having primary custody of her son seemed to suit Gina.

I always had the sense that Gina did not particularly like motherhood and that being a single mom had been hard for her. Gina actually seemed much happier with Brandon and me having custody and being able to visit with Antonio. It is what made her episode with the sleeping pills harder to understand. In most aspects of her life, Gina seemed happy with how everything had worked out. Things were actually better for her. Or so it seemed.

After about a half-hour, Brandon suggested that he and Antonio go get a snack in the cafeteria so his mother and I could have some "girl talk." It was an excuse for me to see if Gina might share what was going on. I wasn't so sure that Gina would be any more open with me than she would be with Brandon, but we figured it was worth a try.

As soon as Brandon and Antonio left the room, Gina's disposition changed. I could see it in her face. She didn't want me there.

"I know that you probably drew the short straw," she said.

"Pardon me?"

"Look, I know that you don't want to stay and talk to me anymore than I want to talk to you," Gina said.

"We just want to know what is going on," I said.

"I was having a pre-dinner drink and got a headache. I grabbed the wrong bottle," Gina said.

"Really? You expect me to believe that? Gina, you're not a senile elderly person who mixes up her medications."

Gina turned her head and looked out the window. I waited a beat. Then it grew into awkward silence.

"Gina," I finally said, "we just want you to get better. If not for yourself, for Antonio."

Gina didn't bother even glancing back at me. She continued to look out the window. Maybe it was easier to talk to me that way. I didn't really care one way or the other.

"Antonio seems to be doing just fine without me," she said.

"Gina, you're his mother. He loves you."

"I'm not stupid. I can see that he is better off with you and Brandon. I was . . . I'm not a very good mother."

I didn't know what to say. I couldn't really argue with her. Frankly, she wasn't the nicest person, period. But I wasn't going to kick her when she was down.

"Is that what this is about?"

"I don't know what this is about. I should be happy with the way things are, but I . . . I just don't know."

Gina reached up and wiped at her cheek. Because her face was turned away from me I couldn't be sure, but it looked as though Gina was crying. Now I really didn't know what to say.

"Are you okay?" That was all I could think of. It seemed appropriate.

"I think you should leave," she said.

"What should I tell Antonio?"

"Tell him that I'm tired and needed some rest."

I nodded my head. I'm not sure why. Gina still wasn't looking at me. I simply turned and left the room.

I checked in at the nurses station and made sure that she was still under careful watch. The nurse showed me that they had a monitor with a 24/7 camera in her room. Someone was at the nurses station at all times and could keep an eye on her room. Plus, the nurse told me, they still did their routine checks in her room.

The nurse also told me they didn't know how much longer the insurance company would let her stay. Medically, she seemed fine. The doctors had ordered some psychiatric testing. The recommendation would probably be for some sort of counseling.

I thanked the nurse and then texted Brandon. I met up with Brandon and Antonio in the hospital lobby. I told Antonio that Gina was very tired and needed her rest. He seemed okay with the explanation. Yes, Gina was his mother. He did love her, but I think he had learned at a young age not to rely too much on her.

In the car ride home Brandon kept checking his phone. I probably should have let him drive. I knew he was corresponding with board members and major shareholders. It was putting him in a foul mood.

After we arrived home, Antonio put on his pajamas. I watched some television with him while Brandon worked in the study. After Antonio was in bed, I went to the study.

"Antonio is bed. He wants you to come say good night," I said.

Branded gave a slight nod of his head as he texted on his phone.

"Brandon, did you hear me?"

"Yes. I'll be there in a minute," he snapped at me.

"Whoa. Hold the phone. I know you are stressed . . ."

"I said in a minute."

I couldn't every recall Brandon being short with me like that. I crossed my arms over my chest and stood in the doorway. I looked straight at him. I waited for him to notice my stare.

After a moment, he tossed his phone onto the desk. He got up and walked toward the door.

"I'm going up to say good night," he said.

I remained where I was with my arms crossed.

"What?" he asked.

"You know what," I said.

"Ashley, if I knew I wouldn't ask."

"I shouldn't have to tell you. You should know." I whirled around and walked away.

"Ashley, I'm not a mind reader."

"You don't have to be a mind reader to know that you're being an ass!"

"An ass?! In what way am I being an ass?!"

"Again, I shouldn't have to tell you. You're a smart guy. I'm sure you'll figure it out."

I walked down the hall and into the kitchen. I heard Brandon walk down the hall and up the stairs. Did we just have the start of our first fight as a married couple? Brandon and I had certainly argued before. I even left him once when he cheated on me while we were dating. But this little argument seemed different.

It was different because we were married now. It was different because his entire tone and attitude in the study were different from anything I had experienced with him before. It was a tone and an attitude that I didn't like. It worried me.

Chapter 36

I sat in the kitchen having a glass of wine. Brandon came in a few minutes later.

"I'm sorry," he said.

"Brandon, do you even know what you are sorry for?"

"Give me a break, Ashley. The company is falling apart. I'm probably out as CEO and my grandmother as President of the company."

"Don't you think that I know that? Brandon, I know that. I understand what is going on. But worse than all of that is that you are shutting me out."

"I don't mean to."

"But you are. And the way you acted toward me in the study a few minutes ago . . . is not acceptable. We are husband and wife. Do you remember that means for better or worse? Richer or poorer? Whatever happens, we are in this together."

Brandon now realized how he had acted. There was the flash of recognition on his face. I'm sure he was also thinking that I was overreacting a bit. Well, I couldn't help it. I felt very emotional.

"I was short with you. I apologize. But, Ashley, I'm not trying to shut you out. I just have a lot on my mind. I have been making calls, texting, emailing . . . I'm trying to touch base with as many stakeholders as possible to see if I can head this all off at the pass."

"I know. I guess I'm sorry as well. Perhaps I overreacted a little."

"No. You're right. I can't wall myself off."

"I'll tell you what," I said. "Antonio should be asleep by now. It's dark out. Why don't we go for a little dip in the pool?"

"That doesn't sound like a bad idea at all. I've done all I can tonight. It's pretty late on the east coast. I'll grab our suits," he said.

"I was thinking that we go without suits," I said.

"Even better," Brandon replied.

Chapter 37

"Okay, buddy, let's get a move one," Brandon called out to Antonio.

We had just finished our breakfast and Antonio was brushing his teeth. Antonio came bounding down the stairs and grabbed his backpack from his cubby in the mudroom.

"All set," Antonio said.

"Have a good day," Brandon said as he kissed me.

"Eww," said Antonio.

"You'll change your tune one day," Brandon said to him.

"I bet you'd like a kiss from Miss Chelsea," I teased.

Antonio turned three shades of red.

"I'll be in the car," Antonio said. He opened the mudroom door to the garage.

"Have a nice day. I love you," I called out to him.

"Love you too," Antonio called back.

"He has a little thing for Chelsea?" Brandon asked.

"You haven't noticed?"

Brandon shook his head.

"Just a harmless crush. It's cute," I said.

Brandon shrugged his shoulders. He gave me another kiss and then followed Antonio into the garage. I heard the garage door open, Brandon's Aston Martin back out, and then the garage door close.

I poured myself another cup of coffee and headed upstairs to finish getting ready for the day. I had finished my shower and was getting dressed when my cell phone rang. It was Brandon.

"Hi honey," I said when I answered.

"I just dropped Antonio off at school when I received a call from Matteo Silvi," Brandon said.

"What did he say?"

"Apparently Gina had a pretty bad drinking problem a few years ago. She got cleaned up, but it had already taken a toll on her modeling career."

"How did we not know about this? Wouldn't this have at least been on the magazine's radar screen?" I asked.

"It probably came across the news wires, but staff writers and editors wouldn't have deemed it a newsworthy story at the time. At that point Gina was only getting small modeling assignments in Italy. She was no longer fashion world newsworthy."

"Okay. I guess I can see that. So, it is fairly safe to assume that her latest episode is related."

"Yes, but there's more," said Brandon.

"What else did Matteo discover?"

"Gina has been estranged from her parents for fifteen years. They were very much against her having a modeling career. Get this," Brandon paused for dramatic effect before continuing. "Gina was a novice in a convent."

"What?! Gina was going to become a nun?"

"Yep. She left the convent and announced she was going to be a model. Her parents pretty much disowned her."

"Wow. That seems pretty harsh and extreme for them to disown her like that," I said.

"According to Matteo, the parents are very devout. Gina has a brother and several uncles who are priests, a sister who is a nun, and one of her uncles is even a bishop," said Brandon.

"Okay, so Gina has had it a bit rough. Actually explains some things."

"Matteo also told me that she tried to reconcile with her parents after Antonio was born. They were even more enraged at her for having a child out of wedlock. When her career completely fell apart this year, she devised the plan to have the annulment certificate removed from the records and come after me for money."

"Wow."

I realized that I was beginning to say that a lot. But, gee wiz, Gina's life was like a soap opera.

"Well," I continued, "that would actually explain a lot. Sort of puts things in perspective."

"Yes. I guess it does. But there is more. Gina's mother died the other day. She learned about it from one of her siblings. She was also told, under no uncertain terms, was she to come to Italy for the funeral. I think that pushed her over the edge."

"She started drinking again and took the sleeping pills," I said.

"But not enough to kill herself," Brandon said.

"A cry for help."

"Looks that way," said Brandon.

"Why didn't she just ask for help?"

"Gina was not used to getting help from anybody. She probably didn't expect to get any this time either."

"That needs to change. Brandon, we need to get her into the best rehab program we can find. Let's get her the help she needs. She is Antonio's mother and it is the right thing to do."

"Agreed. Let's talk to her doctors and get her in a program," said Brandon.

"I'll take care of that. You have enough on your plate at the moment," I said.

There was a pause on the other end of the phone. The turmoil with the board of directors weighed heavily on Brandon. I knew that the Davenport Media board was still a touchy subject.

"I'll talk to you later," Brandon finally said. His voice fell flat. Then the call ended.

Chapter 38

I knew how upset Brandon was about the board of directors. I also knew that nothing productive would come from talking to him about it until we knew more about what might happen. He knew that he could talk to me if he wanted. I left it at that for the time being.

I called the hospital and made an appointment to meet with Gina's doctors. The earliest I could get was the next afternoon. In the meantime, the hospital reassured me that she was under careful watch and receiving excellent care. We were the closest thing that Gina had to family – apart from her actual family who had disowned her. The irony of it all was not lost on me.

I managed to get some work done for the foundation before lunch. I headed into the kitchen to make a sandwich when Brandon's grandmother called me. Jacqueline Davenport was a woman whom I admired very much. She was the reason that I first got interested in fashion media.

As I answered her call, I thought back to the first time that I met her after Brandon hired me as the Director of Social Media for *Jacqueline* magazine. She and I hit it off from the very beginning. She had remained one of my biggest cheerleaders.

"Hello Grandma Davenport," I said as I answered the phone.

"Hello, dear. How are you?" she said.

"Hanging in there. How are you?"

"Hanging in there as well. I do want to discuss the matter of the board with you, but, first, how is my precious great grandson doing?"

"Antonio is the one member of the family who is doing fabulous. He has taken very well to Santa Barbara Academy. He is doing great in his classes and making friends easily," I said.

"Excellent. When all of this business with the board is settled, I must come for a visit."

"You know you are welcome any time," I said.

"I know, dear. You are so sweet. It would be wonderful to spend time with the three of you. I miss you so much."

"We miss you very much as well."

"Then it is settled. As soon as I knock some sense into these idiot board members, I'm coming for a visit."

"Let's hope that is soon. For many reasons," I said.

"Yes. I know how troubling all of this foolishness is to Brandon. It must be causing an awful strain," she said.

"It is very hard on him. There is certainly considerable stress and tension. Just a lot going on for us right now."

I knew that she was aware of Gina's situation as well, but we really didn't need to go into that. The poor woman had more than enough of her own to deal with.

"I really wanted to check in and see how you are doing," Jacqueline said.

"I think that I know Brandon as well or better than anyone. Probably better than he knows himself much of the time, but sometimes it is hard to figure your grandson out."

That actually got a slight chuckle out of Jacqueline.

"Yes, Brandon can be difficult to figure out from time to time. When something truly bothers him, he has a tendency to go into his own world. He walls himself off and shuts others out. That is especially true for those he is closest to. I think he does it thinking that he is protecting us," she observed.

"What he doesn't realize is that it makes it harder on us. If we don't know what is going on, it is harder for us to know how to act around him or possibly even help," I said.

"You are preaching to the choir. He has been that way since he was a small boy."

"So what do you make of what is happening with the board of directors?" I asked.

Jacqueline Davenport was an amazingly strong woman. I knew she was every bit as concerned as Brandon, and, yet, she didn't seem to let it faze her.

"It is a very tricky situation. Those old farts seem hell bent on only concerning themselves with our bottom line and the price of our stock. I know they have a responsibility to shareholders, but what they don't understand is that the *Adele* acquisition will be better for the company given a little time. We will be even more profitable and that will only help the price of the stock. They are shortsighted."

"Do you think you and Brandon can find enough support to prevent them selling the company?" I asked.

Jacqueline paused for a few beats. I knew that meant she was not very confident in how the situation looked.

"Ashley, dear, I simply don't know. It is the first time that I have been unsure of how the board will vote. But, I will tell you this. They have a fight on their hands. I didn't want it to come to this, but they are forcing our hand. I'll call in favors where I can, twist some arms, and gain as much leverage as I can muster. Brandon will do the same."

"And if you two lose the vote?"

"I have seen a lot in my many years. I had to overcome a lot when I started the company. Back in those days, people didn't think a woman could run a major company. So I know adversity and overcoming it."

I had no doubt about Jacqueline. She would be crushed to lose the company she started, built, and ran for so many years. But she had perspective. I wasn't as sure about Brandon.

Chapter 39

Even though it consumed most of his time, Brandon and I avoided talking about the Davenport Media board of directors. I felt as though I was walking on eggshells around him. Fortunately, we kept it all from Antonio. He was a very easy going kid, but he didn't need to make our adult problems his.

On the upside, I had met with Gina's doctors and we got her transferred to a substance abuse rehabilitation program in Santa Barbara. Her doctors recommended the facility and its programs as among the very best in the country. I did some research of my own and agreed. Gina had only been there a few days, but was already making some progress.

I was glad when we got to the end of the week. Brandon planned a strategy with his allies on the board all day Saturday. Ethan Bennett had arranged for Chelsea and me to bring Antonio to the Bobcats final practice before the game.

Ethan also gave us the behind-the-scenes tour. Antonio was on cloud nine. As he learned more about football, he was now very much aware of what a star player Ethan Bennett was and how he had already secured a place in the NFL history books. He also got to spend the day with Chelsea. That always brought a smile to his face.

Antonio woke early on Sunday morning and was ready to go. He was wearing his Ethan Bennett Santa Barbara Bobcats replica football jersey and clutched his VIP pass in his hand.

"When can we leave?" he asked impatiently as I cleared our breakfast dishes from the kitchen table.

"Not for a few more hours," I said.

"Dad, isn't it awesome how we get to sit in the owner's box?"

"Sure, son," Brandon replied blankly. He had his face buried in his cell phone.

"Do you think the Bobcats will win today?" Antonio asked. "I think they will definitely win. Ethan is going to throw for like four hundred yards and at least three touchdowns. I also bet he won't have any interceptions."

Brandon simply nodded his head. I could tell he was only half listening to his son.

"Brandon," I said.

"Not now," he replied.

"May I speak with you a moment?"

"Ashley, can it wait?"

"No. I don't think that it can."

"It better be important," Brandon said as he placed his cell phone on the table.

I had held my tongue, but with each passing day Brandon's attitude moved closer and closer to that night in the study. Now was he not only shutting me out, but he was pretty much ignoring Antonio.

"What is it?" he asked as he looked at me.

"Antonio, why don't you go watch the pre-game show," I said.

Antonio bounded out of his chair and left the kitchen toward the family room.

"I thought we had already been over this," I said.

"Over what?"

"This. Your attitude. I know you are under a lot of stress, but you can't ignore your son."

"I wasn't ignoring him."

"You weren't actively engaging with him either. You weren't giving anything close to your full attention when he was speaking to you."

"Ashley, I am the CEO of a major corporation. A CEO under attack from many of his own board members. I think I can be excused if I don't have time to talk about a stupid football game right now."

I crossed my arms. I always crossed my arms whenever I got really ticked. It was how Brandon knew that I meant business.

"Okay, look, I know you are pissed. But, Ashley, I really don't have time for this conversation at the moment."

"Is that so? When do you plan on making time? And not just to have a conversation with your wife, but to be present to your son?"

"I really can't do this now." Brandon picked up his phone and stood from the kitchen table.

"Don't you dare just walk out of this room," I said.

"Ashley, I said that I can't do this now. I meant it. So, yes, I am leaving the room. I have work to do."

"What about the game?"

"Send my regrets," Brandon said as he walked out of the kitchen.

I followed him into the hallway.

"You're being a real ass!"

"Ashley. I can't deal with the board and you at the same time. I'm sorry. But one crisis at a time is all I can handle."

"Funny, I thought I was your wife. Not a crisis to be dealt with."

"You know what I meant."

"No. I don't. You haven't said enough to me this past week for me to know what you meant."

"This conversation is over," said Brandon as he stepped into his study.

"You can't dismiss me like I am one of your employees. Brandon, we have a real problem if we can't talk to each other."

"The only problem is that I need more time to deal with the board of directors. That is all that matters at the moment. The rest, I am sorry, will just have to wait."

"Why don't you try explaining that to Antonio?"

"He's a smart kid. He'll understand."

"It's not a matter of how smart he is, Brandon. This has to do with sharing something with his dad. He is so excited about the game today."

Brandon wasn't even looking at me any longer. He was replying to a text message.

"Well, unfortunately, he will have to be disappointed by me today. I'm leaving for New York."

"What? Today?"

"Yes. Now. It's clear that I'm not going to be able to get much more done if I stay here. I need to be in New York so I can deal with this."

I didn't know what to say. Yes, the board of directors was important, but Brandon decided he needed to go to New York that minute to what? Escape his family? Get away from his wife? He refused to have a conversation with me. I fought back tears. I didn't want to upset Antonio.

"You have to tell Antonio. I won't do your dirty work for you," I said.

"Fine. I'll text you when I get to New York."

That was that. Brandon stepped passed me and headed for the family room. I ran to the bathroom to cry. After I got it out of my system, I calmed myself down and washed my face.

When I came out of the bathroom, I noticed that Brandon's study was dark. It didn't surprise me that he left without saying goodbye or giving me a kiss. I knew that he gave me the only goodbye I was getting when he brushed past me as he left his study. I took a deep breath and headed down the hall toward the family room.

Chapter 40

I put on a brave face for Antonio. He was disappointed that Brandon had to leave on such short notice, but seemed to be handling it well. Maybe he was putting on a brave face for me.

I sat with him on the couch and watched some of the pre-game show with him. It was a lot of sportscasters and former players and coaches speculating about all the upcoming games and making their predictions for who would win. Most of them picked the Bobcats to win and said that Ethan should have a very good game. I guess that was something.

The Bobcats did win the game and Ethan did have a very good game. I knew that Antonio missed having Brandon there with us, but he had a great time. He was in complete awe of the crowd and being up high in the owner's box.

Antonio soaked it all in. He also made sure to sit between Chelsea and me so he could give us his own color commentary on the game. I also think it had a lot to do with wanting to sit next to Chelsea.

Ethan joined us at the house for dinner following the game. Antonio made sure that we took several pictures of him with Ethan so he could show his friends at school the next day. After dinner, Ethan asked Antonio if he wanted to go into the yard and toss the football around with him. Antonio was out of his seat with football in hand as quickly as Ethan got the words out.

"He is definitely a keeper," I said to Chelsea as we looked out at Ethan and Antonio in the backyard.

"He is pretty special," she replied.

I just nodded.

"Okay, tell me what is going on," Chelsea said.

"Chels, I don't know what to do. It's like Brandon and I can't even talk to each other. He is so wrapped up in the business with the board that he has completely shut Antonio and I out of his life."

"Did you try to talk to him about it?" she asked.

"Yes. We just ended up arguing. Well, sort of. He didn't even want to talk enough for us to have a proper argument. That's what bothers me most."

"That you are not communicating?"

"Yes. I expect for us to argue. Not a lot, mind you, but it is part of being married. I would rather he stayed and argued with me. Instead he just fled. He used going to New York as an excuse to leave."

"I know it's upsetting, Ash, but you two will work it out. Brandon loves you. He lost you once, he knows how lucky he is to have gotten you back. He's not going to screw things up again. Especially now that you are married. I don't see anyway he would just throw that away."

"You didn't see him, Chels. It was like he couldn't even be bothered with me. Or with Antonio. He's obsessed with the upcoming board of director's vote. It's like it has completely consumed him. It's not healthy. It's not healthy for him and it is hurting our family."

"I get that. But maybe he just needs a little time to think. I bet he is doing a lot of that right now."

"I wish that I was as confident of that as you are. I just had never seen him like this before. I didn't even recognize the man that I fell in love with and married."

"He's still there, Ash. Just give him a little time."

"I hope you are right," I said.

"Hey, have I been wrong yet?"

"A few times," I said with a slight smile, "but usually not about the important stuff."

"Then trust me. This may be a bump in the road, but that's all that it is. A bump in the road."

Chelsea put her arm around me and pulled me close.

"Thanks," I said. "I don't know what I would do without you."

"Luckily, you'll never have to find out. BFFs for life. Remember?"

"How could I ever forget?"

I had never doubted my relationship with Chelsea. I was looking for the same confidence about my relationship with Brandon. I should have more faith in my own husband and our marriage. I knew that. I was just scared. I couldn't imagine my life without him.

Sunday afternoon I had received a brief text from Brandon when he had landed in New York. I received another brief text from him later that evening to say good night to Antonio and to tell me that he would contact me in the morning. That was it.

I picked up my phone several times to call him. To text him. To try to break through whatever it was we were going through. Each time I just put my phone back down. I couldn't bear the possibility that my call or my text might go unanswered. That I might be ignored again. I cried myself to sleep.

Chapter 41

Monday morning I dropped Antonio off at school and went straight back home. Chelsea called to check on me and see if we could meet later to go over some of the legal documents for the foundation. I told her I was doing better. It wasn't very truthful, but I didn't feel like talking. Not even with Chelsea.

I did make plans with her to come by the house for lunch. We could go over the papers then. I hoped that Brandon would have called by then. Maybe things would be better.

At about ten o'clock my phone rang. It was Brandon. I was expecting him to call, but the phone's ringing still startled me. I was nervous. It was absolutely insane, but I was nervous to speak with my own husband. My heart was pounding and my hands were sweaty.

I hit the "Answer Call" icon on my phone's screen.

"I'm sorry," Brandon said. "Before you say anything, just let me talk. I was a jerk. I realize that now. I was, as you had so eloquently put it, an ass. I apologize and I promise to make it up to you and Antonio. I love you. I love you both."

"I love you too," I said. I could feel myself beginning to cry. But they were tears of relief and joy.

"Look, Ashley, I know that I became overly obsessed about the board of director's vote. I let it get in the way of everything else. Even after I had done all that I could, when I knew that there was nothing left for me to do, I couldn't let it go. Not for a minute. I did a lot of thinking on the flight here yesterday. I thought a lot more about it last night. I wanted to call you then. But I felt so bad. I didn't know what to say."

"Brandon, it will be okay. I was very upset. This whole ordeal has been very upsetting. What made it worse is that you hurt me and you couldn't even see that. And you disappointed your son. Fortunately he ended up having a great day yesterday, despite that."

"Hurting the two people who I love the most in this world is what bothers me most. I will never let that happen again."

"I can forgive you. I do forgive you. And I know Antonio will be okay as well. But you do need to understand that we need to be able to communicate with each other. You can't just shut me out. No matter what you are dealing with. We are married. For better or worse. I'm not your wife just when things are going well. We deal with everything together. Do you understand that?"

"I do now. Two very wise women in my life set me straight."

"Did your mother and grandmother talk to you?" I asked.

"You're half right. My grandmother and I talked last night. But I was thinking of you and my grandmother. Despite how it appeared, I have heard you. I was listening. It just took a little while for me to get a clue."

I wiped the tears from my face.

"Better late than never," I said.

"I suppose. But I am going to work on getting things right the first time. I need to go in a minute. The board of directors is getting ready to vote. We will learn what our fate is. But, Ashley? . . ."

"Yes?"

"No matter what the vote is, we will be okay. I know what matters most and I love you very much."

"It's good to hear you say that," I said. "Call me when the meeting ends."

"I will. Then I'm coming straight home."

"Good luck," I said.

We ended our call and I tried to keep busy. An hour later Brandon called back. He said that the board meeting had been very contentious. He and Jacqueline had no idea how it was going to turn out. It looked like it could go either way. Nonetheless, they had the necessary votes to retain control of the company.

"Brandon, that is wonderful news. I know you said that we would be okay no matter what, but I am glad that the vote turned out the way that it did," I said.

"Me too. What is even better," he said, "is that the board members who had voted against us were so upset at the final vote that they resigned as a group. Their seats will be filled with more reasonable people who want to support the direction the company is taking, rather than trying to tear it down."

"Well, this calls for a celebration. When are you leaving?"

"In a few minutes. The car is on the way to pick me up. I'll see you later this afternoon. I love you."

"I love you too. I'll see you when you get home."

When Chelsea came for lunch, I asked her if she would pick Antonio up from school and take him out for pizza. I wanted a little alone time with Brandon when he got home.

***

Brandon opened the door and I stepped toward him. He closed the door and took me into his arms and kissed me. We spent the afternoon lounging by the pool, deep in conversation and playfully swimming like school children. All was right with our world again.

Chelsea returned home with Antonio and I looked around at the people I loved and was thankful for what I had in my life. Brandon kept his promise to me. He got it right. Not all the time, but most of the time. And he never shut me out. We were stronger together.

Gina did extremely well in rehab. She worked through those things that were troubling her. She understood herself better. Antonio was still better off living with us and we were a happy family, but Gina became a better mother. She was able to be around more and be part of our family life in a positive way.

Jacqueline made certain she came for her visit. In fact, Brandon's parents came along with her. We had one big family vacation to Disney. And nine months later we welcomed Charlotte Jacqueline Mitchell into the world. Antonio wanted a baby brother. Nonetheless, he was excited to be a big brother to Charlotte.

Four years ago I was swept off my feet by Brandon Mitchell and I fell head over heels in love. Our relationship had been tested, even broken once, and tested again along the way. But we are stronger today.

The Mitchell family will be just fine. I am married to the man of my dreams and we have a wonderful family together. We couldn't be happier or more in love. A love, a marriage, and a family to last forever.

****

Would you like to read another sweet romance?
Start reading *Finding Mr. Right*
(Turn the page for a preview of *Finding Mr. Right*)
- OR -
visit my website for a list of all my Sweet Romance books:
www.elliejadamsauthor.com

Preview of Finding Mr. Right

CHAPTER 1

Justin Renaud sat at his desk flipping paperclips into a cup. He was bored out of his mind. He hated his job. When he graduated with a degree in business he thought he would do more with it than calculate numbers on a spreadsheet all day.

"Renaud, you have those reports for me yet?!" yelled Chris Roberts, Justin's boss, as he made his way toward Justin's cubicle. The only thing worse than the job was working for Chris. His boss was in his early sixties and stuck in a middle manager position he didn't like.

Is that my future? thought Justin.

"I just emailed them to you," said Justin once Chris reached his cubicle.

"Did you double check the formulas?" asked Chris.

"Yep. We're good to go," replied Justin with a deadpan tone.

"It looks like we aren't giving you enough to do," said Chris as he looked at the pile of paperclips near Justin and those in the half filled cup.

"Can I help it if I'm a wunderkind?" Justin flashed a fake smile.

"You can help with the attitude. I get the distinct impression you don't like working here."

"You are very perceptive, Chris."

"Well, there are lots of guys who'd love to have your job."

"Then why don't you give it to one of them? I quit," said Justin as he stood up and walked past Chris.

"Wait just a second," called Chris. "You think you can just up and leave like that? Well, you can forget a recommendation."

Justin had removed his tie before he reached the end of the hallway. He hated wearing ties. They felt too restrictive. It was a symbol of his job. A job he just quit.

Justin stepped out front of the building of his former employer and pulled his cellphone out of his pocket. He called his oldest brother Andrew. A call that was long overdue.

"Justin," answered Andrew. "What's up little bro?"

"I want to talk to you about opening the restaurant. I just quit my job."

"You what? Justin, was that the best move?"

"I've got money saved up. I'll be okay for a while. I just couldn't take it anymore. I'm not a nine to five kind of guy. If I had to spend another day in that office, I was going to throw myself out the window."

"I get you didn't like the job, but you know how Dave and Matt feel about the property. We haven't all been able to agree on this."

"All the more reason for me to quit. Now they will see I am serious about the restaurant. I can devote myself full time to it."

"Alright. I'll call them, but I can't make any promises. Let's all have dinner tonight and talk about it."

David and Matthew were Justin's other brothers. The four of them had discussed turning the old family restaurant into a newer, more sophisticated, restaurant. One that would appeal to a younger, professional crowd. Well, Justin had discussed it. Andrew supported his idea. David and Matthew did not.

It had been several months since they closed the family restaurant. Their dad no longer wanted to run it. Just another thing he gave up on when it came to the family.

He walked out on them six years ago. That, actually, was a blessing. All Justin could remember of his parents marriage was how much they argued. Constantly. He wondered if they had ever been happy together. The divorce had been ugly.

In the end, Justin's mom ended up with a fifty percent stake in *Renaud's French Cuisine.* Their dad continued to run it until about a year ago. That's when he announced he was closing the restaurant. He handed over his half of the deed to his sons. Each owned an equal share.

Their mom told them to do whatever they wanted with the property. She had no interest in keeping the restaurant open or dealing with what became of the property. It was a prime piece of Manhattan real estate. Justin and Andrew wanted to open a new, hipper, restaurant. David and Matthew wanted to sell the property.

They had spent the better part of the previous six months trying to make a decision. They remained at an impasse. But they all knew that they needed to do something with the property. It was too valuable to just leave sitting empty.

The Renaud brothers gathered around Andrew's dining room table. Andrew was thirty-four, David thirty, Matthew twenty-nine, and Justin twenty-four. You could tell just by looking at them they were brothers. Similar heights, builds, and faces. Andrew was an attorney, David a financial planner, and Matthew a hotel manager.

"Justin, you need to let go of this idea for a new restaurant. The property is worth a fortune. We need to sell it and move on," said David.

"And a successful restaurant could earn us profits for years to come," replied Justin.

"If it's profitable," interjected Matthew.

"So are you saying I would run it into the ground?"

"No one's saying that," said David. "Matthew and I just don't see it as the best use for the property."

"Drew, help me out here," said Justin to Andrew.

"I think we should let Justin have a crack at this. Look, the three of us don't need the money from the sale of the property. Justin needs something to do with his life. More than that, it's what he wants to do with his life," said Andrew.

"This is the same conversation we always have. Dude, you're not offering anything new," said David.

"I quit my job today. I want to devote myself full time to opening a restaurant," replied Justin.

"You what?! You quit your job? Are you insane?" commented Matthew.

"It was killing me. I hated it," answered Justin.

"Just like dad. A quitter," muttered David.

Justin leaped up and reached across the table. "Take that back! I'm nothing like dad!"

"Sit down before I kick your butt," said David.

"Better bring some help," said Justin.

"Cool it! Both of you!" Andrew said as he sat Justin back down. Justin shrugged Andrew off as he took his seat.

"We can't keep having this conversation. Look what it is doing to us," offered Matthew.

"You're right," said Andrew. "So let's make a decision. You know I'm already in favor of Justin opening a new restaurant. You and David have never been keen on the idea. Why don't we do this . . . we all go in as equal co-owners of the restaurant. We each have skills that are an asset. I can handle the legal paperwork; Dave, you can handle the finances; Matt you can help with hospitality. Justin is a natural people person and is as smart, if not smarter, than any of us. I am confident he can effectively manage the restaurant. If we can't turn a profit in a reasonable amount of time, we shut it down and sell. The property will only go up in value. I don't see much downside."

That was the best effort that Andrew had ever made to convince David and Matthew to back Justin's idea to open a new family restaurant. Justin and Andrew looked at each other and then over at David and Matthew. They all sat in silence for a few minutes. David sat back in his chair and let out a sigh.

"If Matt agrees, I'll go along with it. But you only get my vote if Matt is full in on this. Justin, despite what you think, I believe in you. But Matt has solid experience in dealing with customers. I want to know he will be available to guide you."

"Okay," said Matthew. "But I'm not going to loose my shirt over this. None of us should. We'll need to get the financing for this from the bank."

"We can use the property as collateral," said Justin. "It's worth more than what we'll need for start-up costs. If we had to, not that we will, we could sell and pay the bank back."

"So we're all agreed, then?" asked Andrew.

"Yes," said Matthew.

"Yes," concurred David.

"Well, it looks like the Renaud boys are going to own a new family restaurant," Andrew said.

"Don't screw this up," David said to Justin.

"Get lost," replied Justin with a smile.

David smiled back. Justin was smart and great with people. He also seemed to be charmed. David actually had little doubt Justin would make the restaurant a huge success.

"What will we call this restaurant?" asked Matthew.

"*Renaud's*," replied Justin. "It will help bring in some of Dad's former customers as well as signal a new and fresh restaurant. Plus, simply using our name offers the sophistication I am going for."

Their French heritage was strong. They all spoke the language fluently. The brothers all smiled and nodded. *Renaud's*. Perfect.

CHAPTER 2

I had just returned to New York City from a long weekend in Boston. I had been helping my former roommate find a place to live after she accepted a new job there. Kelly and I had been classmates at New York University and rented an apartment together after graduation. I grew up in Newton, Massachusetts so I offered to show Kelly around Boston.

My trip also gave me an opportunity to visit my family. My parents still lived in the same house I grew up in. I have many happy memories of living there. I had a middle class upbringing in a loving and supportive family.

I'm the oldest of three children. My younger sister, by two years, was away at college. My younger brother just started his sophomore year in high school. He was now officially taller than me. I was bummed about that and he didn't let an opportunity go by to remind me he was five feet eight inches tall to my five feet six inches.

Each of us have brown hair. The similarities end there. My brother is now the tallest. He is also pretty muscular and very athletic. He has handsome blue eyes. My sister is five feet five inches, perfectly proportioned, has brown eyes, but is uncoordinated. I'm slender but more toned than my sister. I'm not as athletic as my brother but faster. I'm a runner.

Most would consider us a good-looking family. My brother always has girls trying to go out with him. My sister is stunning. If she were taller, she could be a model. I guess I would consider myself pretty. Not stunning like my sister, but I still have nice curves.

"It was so nice having you home for the weekend," my mother said over the phone. I promised I would call my parents as soon as I got home.

"Yes, it was a nice visit. I'm still upset Jonathan is taller than me."

"It was bound to happen, dear. He should end up at least six feet tall. He is in a real growth spurt right now."

"At least I still have an inch on Chelsea," I said.

"Maybe you can time your next visit for when she is home on break," my mother suggested.

"I'll be home for Thanksgiving."

"I'm going to hold you to that."

"Okay. I love you. Tell dad and Jonathan that I love them, too," I said.

"I will. We love you, too."

I hung up and thought about getting Kelly's old room rented. I had a great job in advertising at Jacobs & Sloane Advertising Agency, but there was no way I could swing the rent on my own. Not in Manhattan. I wondered if I could convince my best friend from work to move in with me.

Megan Barnes had become a great friend since we started working together at Jacobs & Sloane. We'd become like sisters over the past year and half. We even look very similar. Most people think we are sisters.

Megan was currently living with her boyfriend, but he was moving to London for a new job. He asked Megan to go with him but she hadn't given him an answer yet. She was torn, but I suspected she was leaning toward staying in New York. Her family was here and she loved her job at Jacobs & Sloane. She had a good relationship with Josh, but I didn't think it was at the point where she would move to another country for him.

I decided to give Megan a call.

"Hey Rache," Megan said when she answered her phone. Megan was the only person who called me Rache. I preferred Rachel, but gave up trying to correct Megan. It was a term of endearment and I was used to it from her.

"Hi, Megs," I replied. Her entire family and closest friends called her Megs.

"How was Boston?" she asked.

"Very nice. Kelly found a nice place. She can walk to her office."

"Sounds great. How is your family?"

"They are all doing great. Jonathan has shot up since I saw him last." I left out that he was now taller than me. I was still sore about that.

"Have you decided what to do about London?"

"I told Josh last night that I'm staying in New York," she said.

"How did he take it?"

"He was disappointed, but understood. I think we both knew that I'd decide to stay. He's a great guy, but it's not like we had reached a point in our relationship where either one of us moving for the other makes a whole lot of sense."

"Are you going to try the long distance relationship?"

"No. That's a bit sad, but I've realized the past few months that I don't see myself marrying him. A long distance relationship would be hard even under the best of circumstances. We've agreed to break up when he moves."

"I'm sorry, sweetie," I said.

"We're okay with it."

"Does this mean you will consider renting Kelly's old room?"

"I was hoping you would ask." I could feel Megan's smile through the phone.

"That is so awesome. It's going to be great having you live here."

"I know. I can't afford rent on my own and I like your place so much better than mine."

"Well, now you can start thinking of *my* place as *our* place," I said with a broad smile.

"Yippee! We can work out the details tomorrow."

"Okay. See you tomorrow, roomie."

"Later, roomie."

I was thrilled Megan would be moving in. It alleviated my concern about paying the rent and it would be so much fun sharing a place with her. No sooner had I tossed my iPhone onto the kitchen table then it started ringing. I checked the screen. Roger.

Roger was my boyfriend. At least I thought he was still my boyfriend. We had been dating about three months. Everything was going fine until he found out Kelly was moving out.

He immediately wanted to move in together. I told him I wasn't ready. We had a huge fight and hadn't spoken in two days.

I was surprised at our positions on the issue. I am all about commitment and a relationship. I eventually want the type of marriage my parents have. Roger was worth building a long-term relationship with, but I wasn't ready to commit to living together at this point in our relationship.

"Hi, Roger," I said as I answered the phone.

"Rachel, I'm sorry. I was wrong to get so upset about the whole not living together thing. You're right, we're not ready to take that step. I hope you still want to be with me."

"Yes. Apology accepted. And I'm sorry, too. I can definitely see how you could reasonably assume that living together would be something that I wanted. I am the queen of commitment and relationship."

"I thought asking you to move in together would prove I am committed to you and our relationship," Roger said.

"I realize that. As much as it is important to me, it's also important we don't rush into something we are not ready for."

"I get it. As long as we are good," said Roger.

"We're better than good," I replied.

CHAPTER 3

The Renauds had a great relationship with their bank. Within weeks the bank approved the financing needed. Andrew drew up all the legal paperwork and incorporated *Renaud's*. David called in a favor of an architect friend to assist in drawing up the designs according to Justin's vision. Matthew contacted the contractors he used at the hotel.

Justin had spoken to his mother and she was happy with her sons' decision. She knew how much Justin hated his job and dreamed of running a restaurant his way. It would also transform the old restaurant into something new. Wipe away the last reminder of her life with her ex-husband.

Justin was meeting with the architect to finalize the design of the restaurant. While the architect explained his ideas, he showed Justin how everything could be configured using the design software on his iPad.

"Perfect. Let's make it happen," replied Justin.

"Alright. I think I have everything I need. We'll finish these up and get them to the contractor," said the architect.

"Great."

Justin shook hands with the architect. He then surveyed the now empty space from the second floor balcony. The downstairs would have the main dining room and bar. The balcony was large enough for smaller tables which would offer a birds-eye view of the restaurant below.

Renaud's was now a legal entity and work was beginning. Soon it would be a new restaurant. Different from the one

Justin's father ran for so many years. Justin looked forward to starting a new chapter in his life.

CHAPTER 4

I sat in my office staring out the window at the building across the street. I was thinking about my situation with Roger. I didn't regret my decision about not moving in together. I was looking forward to Megan moving in with me, but my goal was to settle down and get married. *Could Roger be the one?*

"Knock, knock." I heard Charlie Jacobs voice behind me.

Charles, Charlie, Jacobs was the co-founder and president of Jacobs & Sloane. My boss. And a sweetheart of a man.

I spun around in my chair as Charlie stepped into my office. He plopped down in the chair in front of my desk. He had a broad smile across his face.

"I just wanted to stop by and tell you what an outstanding job you've been doing. Janice told me how invaluable you are to her team," he said.

"Thank you, Charlie," I said. Everybody called him Charlie. We were a small advertising agency. I decided on Jacobs & Sloane over the larger Manhattan ad agencies for that reason.

I saw more opportunity to contribute to campaigns and earn my own accounts sooner. I had also really hit it off with Charlie and the other staff when I interviewed with them. It was hard to believe that I had been at the company a year already.

"I wanted to let you know that we are promoting you to junior executive, effective immediately. You will take on increasingly larger roles on the accounts you work on. I suspect a year from now you will be heading your own accounts."

"Wow. I can't believe this. Thank you, Charlie. I won't disappoint you."

"I know you won't. Rachel, you deserve this promotion. You have worked hard and proven yourself immensely talented and more than capable to take on the greater responsibility. The promotion comes with a nice ten percent increase in your salary," Charlie said.

He could tell from the large smile on my face how happy I was with the news. I was anxious to contribute more of my ideas to shaping campaigns. Now I had my chance.

"Your first campaign as a junior executive will be Jacqueline magazine. Janice will fill you in on all the details, but it is one of our largest campaigns to date. Even though you are not heading the account, there is a lot of opportunity to leave your mark on the overall campaign. I think you will be perfect for it."

"I can't wait to get started on it," I said. I was still beaming. *Jacqueline* magazine was a leading fashion magazine and would be a real feather in my cap if I did a good job on the account.

"You'll do great. Congratulations, Rachel." Charlie then got up and headed out of my office.

"Thanks again!" I called to him as he exited.

He offered me another warm smile as he departed down the hall toward his office.

I walked down the hall to Megan's office. She had made junior executive last month. She felt a little bad telling me at the time as she thought I would be disappointed that we hadn't been promoted at the same time. But I was so happy for her when it happened. And I knew my promotion would come along eventually.

I nearly skipped down the hall as I couldn't wait to share the good news that I had been promoted. Megan was just hanging up the phone when I got to her office.

"It must be good news," she said as she looked up at me.

"I just made junior executive."

Megan jumped up and shrieked with joy. She threw her arms around me.

"That is great news! Congratulations, sweetie. You were overdue for that promotion," she said. "We have to celebrate tonight."

"Sounds like a plan," I said. "Dinner and drinks are on me. I want to spend a little of the raise."

"I know how you feel. The extra income is pretty sweet," replied Megan.

I knew that my raise was exactly the same as what she had received with her promotion. We had started at the same time and at the same salary. It was also no secret that the promotion to junior executive came with a ten percent raise.

"I'm going to call Roger and give him the good news," I said.

"Okay. Think about where we should go to celebrate."

"I will," I said. I headed back to my office and called Roger.

"That's great news, honey," he said when I told him about my promotion.

"Can you join Megan and me for a celebratory dinner?" I asked.

"Better than that," he said, "It will be my treat."

"See you tonight," I said.

"Later, beautiful."

Start reading *Finding Mr. Right*

- OR -

visit my website for a list of all my Sweet Romance books:
www.elliejadamsauthor.com

****

Would you like a free story?

Join my Newsletter and receive a Sweet Romance story as my gift to you. You will also receive author updates, new release alerts, and exclusive contests and discounts. Free to Join. No Spam.   Unsubscribe   Anytime.   Join   at www.elliejadamsauthor.com

Newsletter

Join my Newsletter and receive a Sweet Romance story as my gift to you. You will also receive author updates, new release alerts, and exclusive contests and discounts. Free to Join. No Spam. Unsubscribe Anytime. Join at www.elliejadamsauthor.com

Books by Ellie J. Adams

For a complete list of my Sweet Romance books, visit:
www.elliejadamsauthor.com

About the Author

Ellie J. Adams's books have been downloaded over half-a-million times by readers around the world. She is a romantic at heart and likes her characters to find their Happily Ever After. Ellie's books offer moments of drama, humor, and heartache along the way. Her leading men are strong, but flawed, males, and the leading women are sweet, smart, and independent. Ellie writes sweet romance you can get swept up in and takes you away.